That Was

Yesterday

By HJ Bellus

That Was Yesterday

Copyright © 2018 by HJ Bellus.
All rights reserved.
First Print Edition: December 2018

Limitless Publishing, LLC
Kailua, HI 96734
www.limitlesspublishing.com

Formatting: Limitless Publishing

ISBN-13: 978-1-64034-483-9
ISBN-10: 1-64034-483-7

Dedication

To Coach, also known as Brinkley in our family, you my friend, have no idea what an inspiration you are. You inspired my Libs and helped her believe in herself. I know you've done the same to countless others. You will always be a hero in our house! You're also one hell of a best friend; I love you dearly. Here's to several more memories. #itaintmyfault #blameitonthe #roadtriphome #coach #amazingwoman #godyesisnapchatnow

Prologue

"Max!"

Her again. The thought makes me feel like a monster and sick at the same time. She's the one woman I should be loyal to and love without second thought. But it's a tough job. I find myself hating her more often than liking her.

"Max, now," her throaty, smoky voice growls out.

I round the corner, tucking my hands in my pockets. "Yeah, Mom?"

She's strung out on the couch with a lit cigarette perched on her lips while she dangles an empty bottle of Vodka. "Need more booze, son. Go grab me some. Get a carton of Camels while you're there."

"Mom." I glance down kicking the tip of my worn shoe against the corner of the wall. "It's a new town, and remember I'm only twelve?"

I regret the words the moment they leave my lips. I know better than to reason or even talk to my mom when she's in this state. She always becomes enraged.

"You spoiled little shit." She tosses the bottle to the ground and staggers toward me, the cigarette still coupled between her lips. "I've fucking given you everything, and you have the fucking balls to back mouth me?"

As soon as her nasty words leave her mouth, I feel the sting of her palm across my cheek. My hands shiver in the denim of my worn pockets. I know better.

"Get your fucking ass down to that store. I've blown Jeremy enough, and he knows to bag up my goods for you, and if you want to talk back, go for it, you piece of shit."

"Yes, Mom." I glance down to my tattered sneakers that are two sizes too small.

Another sting strikes my cheek then my shirt is ripped, and a searing pain pierces my skin. The smell of smoke and her cackle cause my spine to shiver. Tears threaten to spill over from the pain. But I learned a long time ago: crying only makes it worse.

"Now fucking get gone." She shoves me back, ramming my back into the sharp corner of the wall. "You have twenty minutes before I call the cops."

I keep my head facing down but can't help the smirk on my face. That used to work when I was five. It put real fear in me. Now, I know it's a lie and always has been. There's no way she could call the cops. I wish like nothing else she would. And maybe, just maybe, they might save me.

I kick rocks on the dirt road with each step, keeping my shoulders slumped and avoiding rubbing the pain in my chest. My heart hurts worse than the new burn. It now makes over a dozen of them.

We've moved countless times. It always starts with a paper posted on our door. I soon learned it's an eviction notice. I remember the day I asked my second-grade teacher what the word was. I knew it started with an "e" but couldn't make out the rest of it.

I'll never forget the smile that crossed her face and the unmistakable joy that overtook her features when she explained the concept. It wasn't until a few months later that I connected all the dots. She was thrilled to get rid of me.

We've been in Boone now for two months. Mom has a sweet deal with the owner. He comes over when he feels like it, they shut the door, and lots of sounds come from it. Mom brags all the time about not having to pay rent. It's by far the worst house we've ever lived in, with creaky floors and leaks everywhere. The carpet in my room is nice, though, and makes a soft bed.

"Watch out, kid." A larger boy brushes by me, shoving my shoulder. "God, you stink."

His friends laugh along with the cruel joke. I'd made it to town and hadn't even realized. I keep my gaze focused on the tiny market on the corner, not paying them any attention. I've heard it all.

"I bet he's the new boy. Heard his momma was nothing but a whore," a voice chides from my back.

I keep walking with my head down. Nothing ever comes out of sticking up for myself. The burns on my chest speak for that.

"You deaf?" A hand shoves my shoulder.

Laughter fills the air. "Probably deaf and dumb."

A rock sails through the air, nailing my shoulder.

3

I don't stop. They follow me all the way to the corner, taunting me and tossing rocks. Eventually, they give up when I don't react. I know it won't be the last I see of them. They'll make my school year a living hell. It's pathetic to think I never want summer to end because that's all I have to look forward to.

The bell above the door rings. The aroma of food hits me, reminding me how hungry I am. Since Mom doesn't have to pay rent, she dumps her monthly checks into booze and cigarettes. I clutch the fifty-dollar bill in my hand, wanting nothing more than to buy a hotdog, smother it in mustard, and fill an extra-large cup with cherry slushy.

The crisp bill in my hand is a brutal reminder of the pay from my dad. He pays my mom a hefty sum every month to keep me a secret. It's always been like that.

"Did you all hear Jessie might be coming back to town? Heard his injury is pretty damn bad," a random voice announces.

Endless chatter ensues about this Jessie guy. I run my hand along the row of chips, imagining their salty goodness before making my way to the counter. A neon yellow poster catches my attention.

Summer Football Camp
Hosted by Hometown Legend: Jessie James

I continue reading all the print, growing more and more excited as I do. Sports have always been my one escape, even when it's just me in the backyard tossing a deflated ball against the side of the house after Mom has passed out.

My heart sinks when I read the cost. It will never be an option for me. Mom would never fork over a hundred dollars for her kid to spend a week doing what he loves.

I clear my throat. "Excuse me, sir. I'm here to pick up an order."

I've learned it's best to use code words rather than asking for a bottle and a pack.

"You Max?" The burly man with stained yellow teeth leans down on the counter.

He's for sure my mom's type. I've never understood why she goes for these types of men with big bellies and dirt under their nails when she's the most gorgeous woman I've ever seen. At least she was before she decided to drown herself in booze.

"Yes, sir." I nod, holding out a trembling hand.

"Should've known. You look just like your momma." He bends down, pulling up a brown paper bag.

"Thank you, sir." I nod and eye the piece of paper one more time.

"Go ahead and take one." He pushes one my direction.

"No, thank you."

Embarrassment and shame, a well-known friend, creeps up my spine. I turn before tears really do escape this time. I notice a booth in the corner filled with farmers drinking coffee and talking. One of the men stands up from the booth and extends his hand my direction.

"Hey there, son. I'm Papa."

His warm and friendly greeting shocks me. I'm taken aback. No one is ever nice to me. They stay far

5

away from me, staring at me like a freak of nature. In a natural response, I take a step back.

"I'm Jack. Most people around these parts know me as Papa. What's your name?" He jerks his chin, keeping his hand outstretched.

With a trembling hand, I shake his.

"You must live out on the Conrad place north of town with your momma?"

I nod and shake his hand. The moment the connection is made, I know he's a different kind. There's something about the thick flannel work shirt he's wearing, his kind smiles, and the wrinkles that shadow his eyes.

"Yes, sir." I nod again.

"Well, son, I've paid for a spot at that football camp. Just got news today the young man can't attend. It's all yours if you'd like."

My jaw slackens. I'm shocked by the grace of kindness shown to me. It was one small action. One I had no idea would change my life forever.

"Thank you, sir." I smile for the first time in my life.

I'd have to walk to town and back, which to the school is more than a good mile. But I'll do it.

"If you ever need anything, you come find me out at Jones' farm or ask for me in town, son. And I mean it."

"Thank you," I repeat myself again.

It ended up that I met this man the town hails as a hero, Jessie. He was kind and caring but never showed anyone favoritism. It was the tiny spark that ignited the fire inside me.

Chapter 1

Max

"What's your plans, Pretty Boy?" Adam leans down, lacing up his designer shoes.

I despise that nickname. It stuck after I refused to be called Golden Boy by my new teammates at Michigan. It was no secret who my dad is, Jessie James. This university still treats him like a god.

"Finishing an accounting project and hanging with Ally. You?" I zip up my duffel and relax back on the lockers.

I don't miss the disappointment in Adam's glance. He's not an Ally fan, and neither is my mom for that fact. I've been with her since my sophomore year in high school. Young love that's going to make it.

"Come out with me and some of the boys, man. It'll be lax since we play tomorrow. Nothing wild. Just hanging out and playing some Xbox." Adam rises to a standing position.

I'll never get over his sheer mass and size. The

crazy ass is over six feet tall and two hundred ninety pounds. He's the brick wall that protects my ass on the field and has become my best friend here. Adam knows all about my past and how Jessie and Jules took me in as their own.

"And booze, women, and who knows what else," I add.

He slaps a hand on his chest. "Me? No fucking way, man."

"Get out of here." I stand up and shove his chest. "You're a shit liar."

"Got me there." He holds open the door for us. "But one day when you get your dick untangled from Ally, then I'll show you real life."

I shake my head. Adam reaches over ruffling up my hair, the only fucker who can get away with it, before he heads off to his blacked-out Escalade. Adam comes from money. It's evident in his designer clothes that you'd never find me in. The thing about Adam is you'd never know this fact on the field. He works harder than any other player. He's a one-of-a-kind man.

I weave in and out of rows of cars making my way to my old black work truck, a 1979 Chevy. Worked my ass off for it and damn proud of it. I've been saving extra cash that I don't spend on Ally to fix it up with a new paint job.

My phone rings in my pocket. The pop song blaring lets me know it's Ally. I stop and drop my bag, answering the call.

"Hey, babe."

"Hey." Her bright and affectionate voice causes a wave of love to roll over me.

Ally is her own person, not caring what others think of her. She lives with no regrets, and that's the first thing that drew me to her.

"I'm just heading out of practice. Was going to grab us some pizza and salad for dinner then I'll be at your dorm."

"Um, damn, baby. I'm sorry. I was called into work. I couldn't say no. Remember Sally, who is a single mother? Her little one has the flu."

I run my hand through my messy, dark hair, stopping my hand on the back of my neck and wringing out the frustration.

"Ally, this is like the third time this week."

"I know, Max. I swear I'll come to your dorm tonight after my shift and then I'm all yours."

It's not the best time, but it's out before I can stop it. "Why do you continue to work at that gym? You don't even have to work."

"Seriously, Max." Agitation swells in her voice. "You of all people should understand."

Beats of silence float between us. Adam's recent show of his disapproval of Ally taunts me. We aren't a perfect couple by any means, but I love her.

"Sorry, babe. I'm exhausted and just missing you."

"Ditto." There's rustling on her end of the line, and a slight giggle escapes her before she focuses back on me. "I promise, baby. I'll be there tonight."

There's something in her voice that sends chills up my spine. I'm too damn exhausted to acknowledge it.

"Love you, Ally."

"Love you, too, number eleven, always and

forever."

Then the call ends. College has been hell on us. It's nothing like high school, where we spent all our time together. Ally was always on my arm or by my side. She gave me strength, and I fed off her love. But in the real world, it seems everything is shifting swiftly.

I bend over and grab my bag, tucking my phone back into my worn jeans. The feel of them on my skin soothes me. Jessie and Jules, my mom and dad, tried time and time again to get me new ones. I refused them, loving the feel of worn clothing on my skin. It felt like home and comfort all in one.

I pause mid-step, re-thinking Adam's invitation. There are several doubts lingering in my mind, but being the leader of my football team isn't one. Those brothers are mine. Respect flows through us. When we are on the field, it's about nothing but getting the job done.

I begin texting Adam, letting him know I'll hang at his place tonight. His parents set him up with a pad that is more like a damn mansion most businessmen crave.

"Ssssshhhh, Jack, he's going to hear you. Dad, he ruins everything. Can't you do something?"

I glance up and look around. Jesus, walk throughs must have been a real bitch tonight. I'm beginning to hear things.

"Skew you, Sissy. I see my bubba."

Again, I look around, and that's when I see a blur of dark hair, chubby cheeks, and grimy fingers raised up in the air.

"Bubba!"

I step out into the main path of the parking lot, making sure no cars aim his direction, and crouch down, tossing my arms wide.

"Jack." It's the first sign of happiness in my voice.

He picks up speed, bolting straight toward me. My little brother is nearly six years old and is a tank.

"He ruined it, Dad. I told you he would. He ruins everything." A voice echoes in the background.

I catch Jack in my chest and look up to see my mom, dad, and two little sisters. I've trained myself to never cry, but in moments like these, I let it go. These are my people, the ones who saved me.

It never fails to happen. Every single time I'm lost and wondering what the hell I'm doing, my family is there to pick me right up off my ass. They say blood is thicker than water, but I'm here to tell you that's all shit as I gaze up at my family.

Jessie, my high school coach and idol, made me into the man I am, but it was the woman by his side who made me believe.

Some things never change, and that includes mean and cruel assholes. Freshman year of high school holds a stigma, but for me, it's far worse than that. I've had garbage stuffed in my locker, shit smeared on my PE locker, and tripped five times— all today, the first day of school, and it's only third hour.

I've remained solid and never react, no matter how brutal the punishment. It's the one thing my mom has taught me over the years. I take it all, square on my shoulders. I've been pegged the town trash, and it seems peers and their parents have a great time ridiculing and judging me.

I think about the brand new cleats safely in my backpack. I haven't let my pack out of my touch all day. Those cleats are my everything. Saved every penny and dime I could to buy them thanks to the grunt work at Gravy Dave's. I ain't about to complain since it's the only place in town that would hire me. Hell, I'm not even good enough to shovel horseshit for local ranchers.

The football tryouts are today, and I'm damn ready to endure all the taunting abuse from the boys in my school. It won't stop me. Football became my life years ago. It was a time where I could be me and work out my aggression in a healthy manner. One gesture of kindness solidified the fact that I'll never give up. Papa Jones opened that door for me. He was one hell of a man, always watching out for me until the day he died.

He and his wife, Jane, would invite me over for dinner. He'd give me odd jobs, but I always refused his money. He'll never know what he gave me was far more valuable than cold hard cash.

I manage to make it through the rest of the day with little incident. Well, in other eyes it's more than little.

"Thank you," I whisper to myself when I enter the locker room.

I keep my gaze glued to the floor, studying the swirling patterns in the tile. I don't have a gym locker since Mom couldn't afford to pay the twenty-dollar fee at registration. In fact, it was me signing up for high school being grateful it's a public education system and the costs were all donations. Donations my ass. I was looked down on when I didn't have the money for an activity card or fee for classes.

I managed to save up the hundred-dollar fee for sports even if it was slid across the counter in rolls of coins. Didn't matter to me. I made it happen.

"Trash can, you really don't know when to give up."

A chorus of laughter ensues. I don't look up, digging out my workout clothes from my bag. The used pair of black gym shorts causes a smile to spread across my face. Brinkley, my middle school teacher, always took care of me by sneaking used clothes in my bag and making sure I had stuff I needed. She and Papa Jones always took care of me. Two people out of this one-horse small town.

"Shit," I hiss, reaching back, rubbing the ache from the back of my head.

I hear the roar of laughter. Some jackass took it upon himself to throttle a ball at the back of my head.

I grab the clothes then saunter to a bathroom stall, ignoring all of it, never reacting to their dick moves. I realize my mistake when I make it back out to the main area of the locker room. My bag has vanished as well as most of the players. I have no other choice than to set my worn jeans and thin as hell t-shirt on the bench. I won't let this get me down when I've come this far.

I never played ball in middle school. I didn't have a job then, so there was no way in hell I'd ever be able to pay the fees and get the minimal equipment. It didn't stop Coach Brinkley from helping me in every way possible, even though she was a basketball coach.

"Here he comes." I hear a whisper.

This time, it's a mistake ignoring the taunt. I'm jumped from the back, and before I know it, I'm slammed down in a mud hole near the bleachers. A few kicks land on my sides, then my bag with all my textbooks plops down next to my face. The laughter is deafening, and it's the first time the desire to fight back ignites inside me.

These assholes who have slammed me since Mom and I moved here will not ruin this moment in my life. Something inside of me cracks wide open, and I'm done being everybody's punching bag. I hitch up onto my knees, my palms sliding around in the wet slop.

"Stay down, you piece of trash." Another kick comes, and I'm done.

I fly up, my hands clenched in fists and ready to strike anyone who comes near. Before I have the chance to throw a first punch at any asshole near enough, I'm jerked back by my collar.

Jessie, the head coach, shakes me until he has my attention. He's a god around here and has always treated me with the utmost respect. He encouraged me every year to try out for the middle school team. I'd come up with excuse after excuse. It's well known around these parts that he was and is still in love with Papa Jones' daughter. Heck, Jessie even tried to slip me enough money to cover my seventh-grade fees for football, but I wanted to earn the right to play.

"Answer carefully, boys," he grits out, "because I'm only asking once. What in the hell is going on?"

My knees go weak from the deathly venom spinning off every word. Everyone goes silent. Not one coward steps up. I go to open my mouth to tell him everything is okay but then snap it shut. Because it's not. This is my time. The years I've looked forward to. I'm years away from escaping my mom and living out my passion.

"Why are you so fucking quiet now?" he yells, the veins popping in his neck.

Jessie is known for his passion on and off the field. He makes no excuses for his language and temper when it comes to football.

"Someone better start talking before I really get pissed off."

Cole, the ring leader of all the jocks, steps up and crosses his arms over his chest. He's a junior and the star of the team. "Coach, we were teaching this punk here a lesson. Frankly, we don't want trash like him on our field."

"Is that right?" Jessie lets go of me and strides right through the mud until he's up in Cole's face.

"Yes, that's right," Cole replies.

"What if I don't want a spoiled-ass rich kid on my team? You ever think about that? Your last name only gets you so far in life, Cole." Jessie shoves his chest, standing up to him. "You want to lead this team, but you throw down a teammate in the mud, taunting him. You think that's a good example of leading your team to another championship? I don't fucking think so."

Jessie steps back crossing his arms to match Cole's stance. "Anyone else have anything to say."

"No, sir." A murmur washes over the air.

Cole slays his buddies with a death stare. I have no doubt they'll pay later for their answer.

"You may live in a small town, but not one of my players will think like a small-minded idiot." He walks back over to my side and slings an arm over my shoulders. *"I've been watching Max since he attended his first football camp. And you'd do best to pick up on some of his work ethic, because he has the natural talent to place all your asses on the bench."*

Cole shakes his head and turns his back.

Jessie roars one more time. "Laps the entire time. You stop and I add another hour. You slow your asses down just a tick and I'll add two hours. When you puke, I hope you think twice before pulling a stunt like this again. Fucking run!"

The players drop their helmets and pads and race to the track circling the football field. A foreign feeling creeps through me. I have no clue how to react to this sensation. Someone stuck up for me.

I wipe the mud from my face and turn to the track to join the team.

"Son," Jessie places a palm on my shoulder, *"don't you ever let anyone treat you like that again. You fight back with all you have until you shut them up."*

"Yes, sir." I extend my hand. *"Thank you."*

He nods. I continue to the track.

"What are you doing?"

I turn back and look Jessie in the eyes. "Joining my team."

"Did you hear me?" Little Jack slaps my cheeks. I'm taken back to that moment in the gas station when Papa Jack saved me even though he had no idea.

I shake my head, still shocked as hell. Mom and Dad told me Whit had a regional dance recital this weekend and that they'd be listening to the game on the radio.

I could see it now. Dad making sure Whit had all her glitter and shit while Mom chased Jack around while nursing Emma. It would be a shit show, but the best time ever. Dad would have an ear piece with the game in his ear randomly shouting out about the shit plays and calls.

"No, Junior, I didn't. What's that?" I stand up and bring Jack to my chest.

"We's surprised you and now gonna eat pizza. Lots and lots of it and Momma said we get ice cream, too, cause you playing on the big thingy."

Jules steps up with baby Emma clutched to her chest and runs a hand down Jack's back. "The big screen, little guy."

"Screw football," Whit mumbles, kicking the toe of her Con on the pavement.

"Language," Mom scolds her.

"It's football season." She shrugs her shoulders. The venom of her pre-teen attitude is in full force.

I set Jack at Mom's feet and head to Whit. At one point in time, she was the center of attention and in her own right still is. This girl will never be in the shadows. She's struggling with the tug of war of puberty where she's no longer a baby girl but not yet an adult.

"Hey, Squirt." I ruffle her slicked-back ponytail. I dodge her arm before she has the chance to connect to my sides. "Oh, don't you smile."

"Knock it off, Max!" She swings harder and

17

faster.

I've got size and power on her. She has no hope. The harder she fights against me, the more her smile appears on her face. I take advantage of her stance, grabbing her and slinging her over my shoulder in a fireman's hold.

"Who's the champion? That's right, I am," I taunt, dancing around in the parking lot.

"Put me down, Max. I swear I'm going to destroy you."

"Oh yeah." I lean forward, giving her hope of being set down, then jerk back up. "Gonna get me in one of those dance ninja moves?"

"You're a jerk," she manages to get out between giggles.

I jerk and weave around the parking lot before putting her back down. Before she's able to dart away from me, I whisper in her ear.

"Love you, little girl, sass and all."

"Love you too, Max."

She then promptly steps back, still feigning anger towards Jack. The battle is real between these two. They'll be wrestling and beating the crap out of each other before long.

"Max." Jules is next with one arm held open.

"Mom." I grab her and pull her towards me, being careful of my youngest sister, Emma.

I never thought I'd be able to use the term "Mom" again until Jules and her undying love.

"You look too skinny. Have you been eating? I swear, Max, if you don't drink protein shakes and warm up meals in your dorm, I'm gonna swat your ass."

I close my eyes and let true love sweep in. It's the only thing that has ever warmed me from head to toe. These are my people, and I'll never let go.

"Jesus, Jules, he's a grown man." Dad pushes her away and gives me his sort of one-armed hug.

"Yeah, Wesus, he's a full man," Jack chirps.

Mom shakes her head, and we all erupt in laughter. Even Whit finds herself laughing.

"How did this happen? Whit has competition." Jack tugs at my jeans, so I pick him back up. The boy is nowhere near being a toddler, but it doesn't stop him. Any athlete wouldn't need a workout with this chub around.

"Surprise." Whit waves her hands in the air, pointing to the truck.

That's when I see all the decorations covering my old work truck. My high school number, twenty-four, is plastered all over it with a gaudy mix of my high school and college colors. This has Mom written all over it.

Dad wraps an arm around my shoulder, ushering our family toward my truck. "Knew you were getting homesick and thought we'd bring a little bit of home to you."

I shake my head, not knowing what else to do. It's my second year of college. I should be thriving and not wanting more or missing my family. I came a long damn way and want more than what I have. It's a selfish jerk move. I love football, live for the game and the high I get from it, but I want to make a difference. These thoughts rattle around in my head on repeat, making me second guess everything.

"Son, just breathe. It's gonna be okay." Dad

squeezes me tighter to his side.

He's the only person who knows all my demons and thoughts. You'd think telling the God of football I want more would be grounds for disowning me. Not with Jessie. He loves with all his heart and makes no regrets about it.

"Where's Ally?" Whit spins and twirls in front of us.

"She has to work an extra shift tonight," I answer her.

"What!" Mom halts her step, her voice echoing around the parking lot. "Are you fricking kidding me?"

And here we go. Mom has never cared for Ally. I always found it odd since Jules is one of the most accepting and caring people I've ever known.

"Really, Mom?" Whit plops her hands on her hips. "You can say fricking, but when I do, you act like I've just dropped the F-bomb in church."

She ignores Whit and opens her mouth to give me the same damn speech I've heard over and over. Dad steps in, wrapping her up in his arms and kissing the hell out of her with their new baby safely in their arms.

"Dis-gust-ing," Whit sings out.

Jack follows her lead because that's what he does.

"Come on, you little shits." I usher them into my truck.

Once they're buckled in, I roll down the window, twisting the old school handle, and lean out.

"Pizza on Fifth Avenue." Dad nods.

"Got it," I reply.

They turn, and Dad takes advantage of Mom,

squeezing her ass and never letting go.

"They are so damn gross," Whit announces, knowing I let the little cuss words slip by.

I shake my head, feeling at home even though I'm hundreds of miles away. "It's love, Whit, and you're surrounded by it. Cherish that shit."

"Gherish that shit," Jack chirps beside me with a mile-wide smile on his face, his tiny white teeth shining brightly.

Chapter 2

I roll over in my bed to find a warm body cuddled next to mine. Ally. I brush my hand down her cheek, taking in her perfect features. I lean in, kissing her forehead. This girl has always been there for me. She was the first friend at my side my freshman year of high school and never wavered even when I had to prove myself to my teammates. She held my hand during my mom's funeral and never left.

She rustles around, curling closer into me. I run my hands through her silky raven hair and kiss the tip of her nose. Even though Ally comes from a wealthy family, you'd never know. She has bucked the system at every turn, doing things on her own.

My cellphone lights up with a social media notification. I recognize the time and the game day tag on Twitter. My alarm will be serenading us in less than ten minutes. I reach over and click off the alarm, not wanting it to wake Ally after she pulled a double shift. It wasn't the first time this week. I'll never understand her need to work so damn much.

"You just gonna stare at me?" Ally rolls over until she's settled on top of me with her palms splayed out on my chest.

"Maybe." I squeeze her fleshy hips.

"I'm thinking my MVP has some releasing to do before his big home game." She grinds her center down on me.

And I'm ready. She's wearing a t-shirt with my number plastered on the front. Her full breasts push through the tight shirt. There's no more talking as Ally pulls me from my shorts and sinks down on me. She's always known exactly how to take care of me, and she's nailed it down to perfection.

Minutes later, we kiss under the hot spray of the shower. I drop my forehead to hers and cup her cheeks, grounding myself in my future, clinging onto the little bit of hope I have left inside of me. It deafens out those thoughts of wanting more with my life.

"God, it feels so good being bare inside you." I peck her lips. "Why did we wait so damn long?"

Ally shrugs then wraps her arms low around my waist, resting her cheek on my chest. "I love you, Max."

Odd. Ally is always one to banter back with me with her witty mind. She must be exhausted. I run my hands all over her creamy skin, letting the sweet smell of coconuts and mandarins intoxicate me. It's her smell. I still remember the first day she walked up to me at my locker with that scent hitting me hard.

"You tired, baby?" I cup her face and force her to look up at me.

She nods. There's something behind those eyes,

and I can't quite figure it out. "Exhausted."

I don't say another word, turning off the shower and getting her dried off. I tuck her naked body back into my bed, tugging the blankets up to her chin. "Get some sleep before the game."

"Thanks, Max. You always take care of me."

I brush her wet hair back. "I always will."

"Were you surprised last night?" she asks, rolling over to her side and tucking my pillow under her arm.

"Yeah." I jump into a pair of boxers and pull my suit from the closet. "Good one, babe. The kids missed you."

"I know." Her eyes flutter shut. "I felt so bad, but we have today."

And with that, our conversation is over. I don't know how to explain it, but all I know is there is a tug deep in my stomach that the end is near, and it won't matter how hard I fight to keep us together.

I shoulder my white dress shirt on and fasten my slacks. I hate this part the most out of all the damn hoops we have to jump through for game days. College is a whole new playing field. Back at home, I'd be lying on the couch wrestling with the kids then heading to my truck in gym shorts. The town would have school flags out and the school logo painted in every intersection. That's the football I loved.

I turn to look in the mirror to make sure my tie is straight because I damn well know Mom will chew my ass. I smirk and turn back to Ally before pulling on my suit jacket. Her purse tumbles to the ground, sounding like a damn grenade went off. She doesn't move an inch.

"Jesus, she's out." I bend down to gather up the

24

shit that flew from her oversized purse. I freeze when the baggie comes into view. It's a different one then last time. I roll it over in my palm and glance up to Ally.

Last time, she told me it was her friend's bag of meth and that she was disposing of it for her. I clench the poison in my hand, growing pissed off. I wonder what her excuse will be this time. It's the moments in the shower or waking up next to her that's kept me clinging.

My phone chirps, and I know it's from Coach. I leave her shit on the floor and toss the baggie on the bed next to her. It's a dick move, but the nicest thing I can do right now in the moment. Ally is always the life of the party, enjoying alcohol but never taking it too far.

I perch my hands on my hips and stare down at her. Anger, love, and hurt brew inside me, creating a perfect, awful storm tearing me apart. I bring a hand to grip the back of my neck and squeeze tight.

"I love you, Ally."

My phone goes off, forcing me to turn and walk away. I ignore the temptation to slam the door. I curb all the emotions and confusion inside. The hallways are a ghost town. Won't be the same story in a few hours with game day in full force.

The same flier tacked to a cork board flutters in the breeze. I swear it does every time I pass by. It's as if the fibers in the paper are screaming and calling out to me. In my gut, I know it's the more I want. Need.

I stop this time and read the advertisement for United States Marine Corps.

"Interested, son?" Dad slaps a hand down on my shoulder.

I glance over at him, having no idea where he came from. I remain silent.

"You know it's okay if you are. I'll still love you if football isn't cutting it for you."

I drop my head. "How did you know?"

"Know you better than you know yourself, Max."

"I feel so damn selfish. Do you know how many men my age would give everything up for what I have?"

"Yeah, I do. The day I was forced to give up football, I thought I lost everything." Dad turns, ushering us out the front door. "My life was over or at least I thought it was. I was so damn wrong. The thing is, son, you never know."

"Yeah. I just don't know." I kick a pebble on the sidewalk as Dad walks us over to my truck.

"You will. Listen to your gut." He shoves off me. "Now, give your old man a ride to the stadium."

"How in the hell did you even get here?" I finally snap out of my stupor.

"The kids were all out and your mom was taking advantage of the silence doing some writing, so I grabbed some coffee and walked over here."

"Thanks, Dad." We both climb into the truck.

I tell him everything on the ride over. Everything washes from me in a turbulent cascade of a waterfall from wanting more to Ally. This is long overdue. I should've known I could've come to Dad way before this. He doesn't say a word or physically react. He listens with no judgment like he always has. He promised me a long time ago that he'd never leave

26

my side, and the man has never once wavered on that promise. It was the day I became a man.

"Mom." I toss my gym bag on the counter. "Got your favorite burgers for dinner."

The stale scent of cigarette smoke hits me hard in the face. I've resorted to keeping my clothes outside in a shed so I don't go to school smelling like an ashtray. I'm not worried about being beat much anymore. She's grown ill from abusing her body, and it seems she's made her rounds through all the men in town since none have been over in a month.

They were another story, loving to knock me around. Mom never did anything but sip from her vodka and puff on her cigarette. I've given up on saving her. It's the hardest thing I've ever had to do.

Any second now, she'll growl back in her smoker's voice. The throaty and gravelly deep sound always reminds me of home and where I come from.

"Mom," I holler again. "Got your carton of cigarettes too."

Yeah, I'm still grabbing brown paper bags for her at the gas station on the corner. I plate her burger and fries and make sure to give her three ranch dips to avoid a hostile fit from her. She must've dozed off. Another cigarette burn in the carpet will be the only result of her careless action.

I round into the living room from the kitchen with our food in my hands. I'll go eat outside, unable to stomach the state of my mom and the smell of the house. The plates clatter to the ground when she comes into view.

"Mom," I roar.

Her lit cigarette dangles between her fingers, dangerously low to the carpet. Her head is tilted to the side while the rest of her body is lax. It's the coloring of her skin that sends me into a panic. I race over to her, my entire body trembling in fear.

"Momma." I drop on my knees, grabbing the cigarette and putting it out in an old Vodka bottle. "Momma."

I grab her. She's cold. A dam bursts inside me. I don't recognize the voice roaring around. It's several minutes before I realize it's me. The tender glass inside me shards and breaks into tiny pieces.

I see an empty pill bottle lying next to her. Then her body twitches against my chest. My mom's cold body burns my skin. I grab my prepaid cellphone and dial 911, doing my best to explain everything through my frantic state. I know in my heart she's gone. I rock her back and forth in my arms, kissing the top of her head, praying for her to take her next breath. Gag, cough, call me a name; I'd take anything right now.

I hate her, hate her and love her so damn much at the same time. The tug of war inside me causes my stomach to swirl on repeat. I keep it down. The piercing and scraping sound of the sirens near, and before I know it, my mother's lifeless body is taken out of my arms. No warmth coats my body. No, her cold skin has seared mine with an icy feeling that will linger forever. I rub my chest over all the burn scars and don't even feel a shred of pain.

I hop in the ambulance, staying away from the action as they rip Mom's shirt off and do everything they can to get one single gasp to expel from her body. When I can't handle watching anymore, I bury my face in my hands and pray like I never have before.

They rush her away once we are at the hospital. I lean back against a wall, dropping my head back on it and squeezing my eyes shut. I've never felt so alone before. Pretty damn ironic, considering I've been all by myself my entire life.

Without thinking, I reach in my pocket and dial the number to the one person who I know will always have my back.

"This is Coach."

"Coach," I stutter out.

"Max?"

"She...she killed herself. She's gone." Despair overwhelms me when I bang my forehead on the dingy wall.

"Where are you?" Jessie barks out, and once I tell him, he ends the call.

I'm left feeling empty once again. Not brave enough to study the action in the hospital. There's a frantic tone surrounding me with all sorts of people racing around.

"Max?"

I bring my head down from staring at the ceiling and tuck my hands in my pocket to see Ally from school. We have a few classes together and have done one school project together.

"Are you okay?" She takes a step closer to me.

I can only shake my head then I feel the hot, wet tears flowing down my face.

"Oh, Max." She closes the distance between us, wrapping her arms around my waist and placing her cheek on my chest.

I don't move. I can't. I'm unable to process a single thought besides the fact I'm a fifteen-year-old boy who is shortly going to become an orphan.

Ally squeezes me tighter to her and begins speaking in a hushed tone. "Father God, my heart is broken for Max. My spirit is crushed watching him live out his own pain. Your word is my hope. I pray that You put your hands on Max and guide him. Give him some peace in his life for he needs You right now. Rescue him from this dark cloud of despair. In the name of Jesus, Amen."

I don't have a chance to look down before I hear someone barking my name out. I jerk my head up to see Coach Jessie and Jules running through the doors. Ally steps to the side. I grab her hand, squeeze, and lean down to kiss the top of her head. I have no idea where that came from, but her simple gesture and kind words finally did the trick, warming me and giving me hope.

"Thank you, Ally." I squeeze her hand again, staring down into her deep, whiskey-colored eyes.

She pats my chest. "I'm here for you, Max."

"Ally, let's go," a stern voice floats down the hallway. Her mother and father stand a good ten feet away with an unpleasant look on their faces. It's as if they both stepped in a big pile of dog shit. And there's the reality slap I needed, because just for a moment I felt loved by Ally and could feel myself falling for her.

Jessie grabs me, wrapping me up in his arms. "I've got you, son."

I shatter for the final time, not one whole piece left inside of me. I sob into his shoulder. "She was so cold."

He doesn't say a word and never lets go. I have no idea how much time passes before Jules walks up to us. It's written all over her face and cemented with the slight shake of her head.

My knees go out from under me. But I never fall. Jessie somehow manages to get me to a couch in the waiting room.

"Look at me." He kneels before me. He waits until I do then grabs my face.

"I don't have anything, not even a goddamn mother," I grit out in anger.

"You've got me. You're mine, Max." He squeezes my face. "Do you hear me?"

I manage a nod.

"You'll never be alone."

I kill the engine in front of the stadium. Dad turns to me, gripping his empty coffee cup. "Max, I can't tell you what to do or how it's going to play out. If you want to join the Marines, then do it. If you want to quit football and just go to college, do it. If you want to come home to help with the farm, then do it. The one thing I do know is that Ally isn't in a good space right now. She's not the same girl you fell in love with. As much as I hate to say this right now, she's toxic to you."

"I love her," I admit out loud without thinking.

"Then you need to help her."

Chapter 3

The roar of the stadium as I lead my boys out onto the turf soothes my aching soul. I glance over to the sidelines to see my dad standing with his hands over his chest and a broad smile on his face. He does his best at my home games not to interfere too much. Doesn't mean he hasn't gotten in my face screaming a line of profanity, helping me get in my zone.

It's not needed today. I have way too much frustration to get out. My line protects me all day as we work the ball down the field. One more touchdown and I know I'll be pulled from the game. We are crushing the other team, and my coaches won't want me to get hurt, especially when it's not a conference game.

I call a different play in the huddle.

"Fuck yes." Jameson bobs his head up and down.

"Line, you hold fucking tight. I'm about to sink this game."

We all clap and head to our spots. I ignore the coach barking in my ear. No doubt there will be consequences for this, but I want to play the way I want. Once my men sprint into action, I see Jameson down the field, wide open. I crank back my arm and aim. Once the ball leaves my hand, I catch a glimpse of a defender flying towards me. I'm able to get rid of the ball before he hits me.

I have no idea if I hit Jameson between the numbers until the crowd erupts in cheers. Adam helps me to my feet, shaking his head.

"You're a dead man." He slaps my back.

"In more than one way," I mumble.

Adam was right. Not only are my coaches pissed and sit me the rest of the game, but Dad glares hard at me. He's not impressed, but I don't miss the mischievous smirk that peeks from the corner of his lips.

The second-string quarterback doesn't score in the last quarter. Our defense holds strong. I find myself glancing around the stadium, taking in everything about game day. It's a source of adrenaline I'll never be able to explain, and I will, for sure, miss it. I'll get my job done here, but there's more for me in the future.

After I get my ass chewed six ways to Sunday, I hit the shower and climb back into the damn monkey suit, preparing myself for the media circus that will surely be ready for me. They love calling me the Miracle Kid. My childhood story has been exposed to the nation. I never fought it, but that doesn't mean I love hearing it every time I lead my team to a victory.

"Saw Ally last night." Adam slaps my back as I finish lacing up my dress shoes.

"Yeah?" I stand up, jerking my duffle over my shoulder.

"She was with Cline, leaving the gym after dark. Didn't look good, brother." Adam relaxes back on the lockers.

"She works there. I'm sure the puke was working out."

"Before a game day?" Adam raises an eyebrow. "That's against team rules."

"He's a puke with no respect. Wouldn't surprise me."

"Yeah, keep telling yourself that." Adam turns and walks out, leaving me alone with my thoughts.

Cline came into Michigan gunning for my position. He was notched down by the coaching staff and put on the kicking team. It only made the chip on his shoulder bigger. I've tried to like him. I've chalked it up to one of those people I'll have to try to respect from a distance. He breaks all the rules and parties like he's a damn rock star when he's not even close. Booze, drugs, and sex are his priorities.

I bite down on my bottom lip, centering myself for the camera crew. Walking out, I get a glimpse of my family standing behind them. It powers me through mundane questions I answer after every game. Once they get their fill, they disperse onto the coaches.

"Bubba!" Jack races up to me, wrapping his arms around my legs. I bend down, peeling him off and hoisting him up to my chest.

Dad gives me a stern look then softens it with a smile. He nods and walks up to me, patting my shoulder. "You know your answer. Where your heart is. Chase your dreams, son."

"Great game, Max." Mom leans in for a kiss on the cheek.

Whit stays back, doing her best to be a pissed off pre-teen. That's until I grab her and mess up her hair. She does her best to bat me away, but it's useless.

"Hey." We all glance up to see Ally jogging our way.

She looks like shit. If I hadn't seen the drugs in her purse, my dumbass would've chalked it up to a lack of sleep. Adam's words pierce my anger. I refuse to ruin a weekend with my family, so I tamp that shit down.

"Ally!" Whit squeals, racing over to her. Jack scrambles out of my arms. They love her. Thing is, they love the girl she used to be. Not this one standing in front of me that I no longer recognize.

Jack stumbles over his excitement until he gets his question out, patting her cheeks. "Where-where were you? You didn't sit by us."

Ally kisses his forehead. "I sat with some friends. I was a few rows behind you, squirt."

Whit clutches Ally's hand as the two drop into easy conversation. Mom hisses next to me.

"Bullshit. I was up and down those stairs a dozen times taking Jack to the bathroom. I'm not going to be able to handle this."

"Don't," Dad warns. "Let's enjoy the rest of the day before we fly home. This is Max's story, not ours. He'll handle it."

And just like that, we all fall in unison, enjoying a day of greasy food, park time, and many laughs. I'm not shocked when Ally leaves early, claiming she has a shift at work.

"Another one?" I ask, grabbing her hand but keeping my distance.

"Yeah, but then I have three days off." She reaches up on her tiptoes. I move so her lips land on my cheek. "What's with you, Max?"

She jerks away her hand, and I step back. "Knocked over your purse this morning. Looks like another friend of yours has a drug problem, Ally. Oh, and Adam saw you and Cline together last night. You tell me what's up, Ally."

My words ring cold and calculated.

"You always believe your teammates over me," she hisses back.

And like Ally has perfected, she turns to my family and says her goodbyes. The kids don't pick up on the hostility underneath her shallow shell.

***

The night sky's darkness matches my mood. With the family gone, I decide to drive by the gym. I'm not shocked when Ally's car isn't there. I notice it on the side street of her dorm. It's parked in the shadow of the building, which I find odd. I kill my truck and walk a good block over to it.

Bass of a thumping song fills the air. The next thing I notice is the movement. I see red, not thinking any of my actions through. Before I know it, I'm ripping open the door to her car.

Neither Ally nor Cline notice me. He has her bent over, tugging her hair as he drives in and out of her. Bile rises up the back of my throat. The memories of my friends and family warning me about this strike me hard and fast. I'm a goddamn fool.

I slam the door shut with all my force. The glass of the window shatters. Ally screams, and Cline whips his head my direction.

"Max!"

I shake my head and walk away.

"Max! Come back here please," Ally pleads.

I never once look back and don't regret it, even though I could drop to my knees in heartache, rage, and pain.

Decision made.

Chapter 4

"You have one minute, and if you're not through this course, you'll be running all night long. Do you hear me, Marines?"

I don't glance up and focus on getting through the course, carrying well over one hundred pounds on my back. My knees threaten to give out while my back spasms in sheer pain. I focus on the end in sight, vowing to not let my body give up. It's all mental. I've got this. Those are the words I repeat over and over in my head.

I'm well and alive, with my soul thriving with what it was always searching for. I'm serving a purpose surrounded by others who have my back. I'm a part of something big here.

Once our whole group is accounted for before the timer goes off, there's a collective sigh of relief, and slaps on the back ensue.

"You looked like you were gonna piss your pants, James." Smith slaps me on the back.

"Damn near did when I saw your ugly mug." I

split a wide grin, struggling to catch my breath,
hunched over, sucking in oxygen in long deep pulls.
   Boot camp is no damn joke.

Drumming my fingers on the keyboard of my Mac, I stare up at the framed picture on my wall of Smith and myself in our fatigues. He was a damn goofy bastard, and after serving nearly five years with him, he became my best friend.

The ringing of my phone pulls me from memory lane. I grab the cellphone and, not recognizing the number, I ignore it. These days I only answer four people. Mom, Dad, Whit, and little Jack are the only ones in my life, even though I live a good eight hours away from there and have never returned home. I never want to go back to the place, remembering the person I was and the way I was treated.

My legs grow numb from sitting most of the day designing websites and managing different divisions of my fast-growing company. Running is the one thing that clears my mind and exhilarates me.

I don't stop until my legs give out. I flop down on a bench in a local park. A ten-mile loop where I let go of all the stress that's built up over the day. My phone chirps with a text. It's Whit reminding me about our trip to the cabin next week. Like I'd forget. It's our ritual every other month. It's a four-hour drive for all of us to the family retreat.

It drives Mom nuts I can't go home. That town holds way too many nasty memories, and my greatest fear is retreating back to the beaten boy if I ever return. It may sound silly to some, but serving the military breathed new life back in, and I won't let anything take that away.

My phone rings, and this time, I answer it without looking.

"Whit, you seriously think I'm gonna forget?" A smile graces my face as I tilt my face up to the sun.

A throat clears on the other end. "Is this Mr. James?"

I hang up, not even answering, letting sun warm my flesh. I have no interest in talking to anyone. I've got everything in my life I need. The phone rings right away, and it doesn't stop. It continues until my temper threatens to explode.

"What?" I growl into the phone. I get so tired of all the telemarketing calls anymore.

Once again, a throat clears. "Mr. James."

It's an honor being called by my last name. Jessie and Jules gave it to me the day they legally adopted me. I wanted nothing to do with the past or my mom, even though it ripped a part of me away.

"Max," I correct the woman on the other end just to be an ass.

Her voice quakes with nerves. "Max, this is Kate Wilson-Valentukonis."

"Kate who?" I bark.

"Just call me Kate." There's rustling on her end then the sound of a door slamming. "I'm the kindergarten teacher at Valley View Elementary."

"Good for you." It's out before I can take it back. I slump forward, resting my elbows on the top of my thighs. Sometimes I think Mom is right and I need to socialize more. I'm becoming quite the hermit. A contempt one, but my social skills are severely lacking.

My snide comment doesn't stop her determination. She doesn't even waver.

"The reason I'm calling concerns one of my students. I'm breaking all kinds of rules and ethics here, but he needs help."

I stand, confused, and pull off my damp shirt then place the phone back to my ear. Once it's slung over my shoulder and there have been a few beats of silence, I'm the first one to speak up.

"How does this concern me? Pretty sure, darling, you have the wrong number."

"This is not a joke. It concerns Finn Ellington. You're listed as his father on the birth certificate, and he needs help."

My world freezes. Not even my worst nightmares have near the power those words do to bring me to my knees. Ellington…that's Ally's last name. A name I haven't heard or spoken since the day I left Michigan after the last home game.

"Finn," I whisper. It's the name Ally claimed she'd name our little boy. It was nothing profound, just the name of her favorite character from *Glee*.

"Yes, Finn. He's my student and has recently been removed from his mother, Ally, by CPS for the third time this year. This time, it doesn't look good. He's going to be put in the system. I just thought, well, I thought maybe you could help him."

"Kate, was it?" I grip the back of my neck, grinding my teeth together. "I don't have a son."

"You're listed on the birth certificate as the father."

"Are you sure?" The question sounds idiotic as it leaves my mouth.

41

"Yes, I am. And I figured you could help."

"There's no way I have a son with Ally. I'd know."

Wouldn't I? I ask myself silently.

"I haven't seen her in six years," I blurt out.

"Finn is five," she whispers.

Silence floats between us for a long time.

"I don't have a son. I can't help you." I end the call and pace back and forth.

The time lines up, his name, and my world blurs. I dial a number on my phone.

"Max."

"Dad."

Chapter 5

Four miles. I drum my fingers on the steering wheel of my old truck. Three miles. My foot nervously taps out a beat. The music playing on the radio is all I can focus on as I ignore the mile markers leading me back to Boone. The place that destroyed, and made, me.

The edge of town nears in my sight. I keep my focus down the two-lane road, ignoring all the familiar sights. A siren sounds, then red and blue lights flood my rearview mirror.

"Son of a bitch." I ease the truck to the side of the road. So much for sneaking back into town unnoticed.

I slam the steering wheel with the palm of my hand. I have no clue how fast I was even going. I slump back in the seat, waiting on the officer. He takes his sweet time sauntering up to me. I study his movements in the side mirror, a habit I picked up in the military. I'm not active anymore, but there are just some things that will never change. I size him up

43

from head to toe. His buttoned-up uniform shirt hugs tightly across his pot belly. There's no way in hell this fool could outrun any criminal, not even a senior citizen. He's out of shape as they come.

"I'm Officer Tomlinson." He rests his hand on my door. "Do you have any idea how fast you were going?"

You've got to be shitting me. Cole Tomlinson, the puke that made my life a living hell from the moment I moved into town.

"No idea." I shrug.

It's then he also recognizes me. "Well, well, the golden boy turned hero has graced us with his presence."

I don't respond, clenching my fist over and over down by my leg. I'd give anything to lay this asshole out. I keep firm in my determination and self-control. I've been through worse these past few years; I can put up with this nobody who thrives in a small town only on his last name.

"You still dumb silent like years ago?" He leans into the window with his stained yellow teeth on display.

"I have no idea how fast I was going, Cole." I lean right back into him. "Give me the damn ticket and go fetch yourself a doughnut, and let's get on with our day."

Cole chucks his head back, letting an evil chuckle escape him. I watch out for each of his moves, letting the plays of the game reel before me. I'd love more than anything to beat his smug ass to the ground. The game of football and the military have taught me better, and if I was man enough to admit it, the times

Mom knocked me around did too.

"Here." I reach over to the jockey box, snagging my registration and insurance, then pull my driver's license out of my back pocket.

Cole steps back and clicks the tiny speaker on his chest. He plays out every single word. It's not the lingo he's supposed to use. Nope, he lets the entire town know I'm back. I can guarantee all those households that have radios in them are garnering smiles right now.

"Station, this is Officer Tomlinson. I have Max James here. He was going fifty-five in a thirty-five. It seems he's still above the law. Writing a ticket for excessive speeding as a welcome home gift." Then he saunters back to his patrol car.

I drop my head back and squeeze my eyes shut. Nothing like ripping off the Band-Aid. Cole takes his sweet-ass time. I ignore the traffic that slows down, staring like they have nothing else better to do.

"I'm writing you up for excessive speeding," Cole rattles on with the rest of his shit speech.

I glance over at him and snag the ticket from him. Tamping down my anger, I decide on the least of several evils and crumble up the ticket in my palm and toss it to the passenger seat.

"Anything else, deputy?" I reach for the steering wheel.

Cole's face turns a shade of red, his own temper flaring to life on the inside. I know I'm playing with fire and gasoline here. Cole may not be the sheriff in town, but I damn well know he will play dirty with the bit of power he does have.

He rests both of his hands on top of my door, his

dirty fingernails resting on the inside. He rocks back and forth for long moments before talking. "You know Jessie and his do-good family may have wanted you in this town, but just know this, Max James."

He sneers my last name with hate and disgust. It's the one thing that nearly ignites my temper to a boiling point. It's the greatest gift Jessie and Jules gave me. I continue to stare forward, not giving him a shred of respect. He deserves none.

"The town doesn't want you here and never has wanted trash like you and your drunk of a whore mother." He pats the top of the door and steps back. "Have a nice day and welcome home, Max."

"Fuck you," I mutter under my breath, no longer able to control shit.

Cole freezes and tilts his head. "What was that, soldier?"

He threw the goddamn bait, and I took it.

I shake my head and pull my ball cap down a bit lower. "Have a nice day, Deputy."

With that, I start my truck and pull back onto the main road. I control my breathing and fall back into my self-disciplined ways. I know men like Cole aren't shit in the real world. He lives safely in the cocoon of this small town where his power means something. He wouldn't last one minute out there.

"Why do you let those motherfuckers have any control over you? They're nothing."

I smile, thinking about what Smith would always tell me when we'd share stories about our hometowns and pasts. I find myself driving without thinking.

Before I know it, I'm killing the engine of my truck in front of my childhood home. One of several, but it was the place she died. The shamble of a shack is barely standing, but the memories it holds are alive and well.

The cracked, barely there sidewalk is no longer visible, hidden by the thick weeds. As I walk, up to the front door, I rub my chest, feeling the burn of the pain this place brings back.

Nobody moved in after Mom took her life. It was tainted that day and wasn't in any kind of living condition.

"How did my life come full circle?" I ask everyone and no one at the same time.

My phone dings in my pocket. I let it stay there, thinking about what in the hell I'm going to do. If I'm being honest, I haven't been able to think about the possibility of having a kid. It's not that I'm opposed to it. The problem is every time I go there, I grow so fucking angry at Ally. What in the hell was she thinking? If that boy is mine, there's no way in hell there's any excuse for what she did.

I pull my phone out and see a text from my dad.

Dad: You in town yet? Let us know.

I tap back a quick response, letting him know I'll be home in a couple of hours. I need time to process all of this. Dad looked into the claim Kate dropped on me. He said it was damn well possible the little boy was mine. He found out that Ally moved back to the area about five months ago.

She's not in Boone but the neighboring town of

Morton about twenty miles away. Her parents have disowned her. The chatter around Boone was she ran off with a guy they didn't approve of, a likely story everyone would believe.

I stand up and dust off my ass, walking around the house. Once at the back, I notice the door is wide open, hanging off its hinges. I glance inside, seeing the hallway that leads directly into the living room. The place my mom drank herself to death, screwed random men, and ordered me to go buy her more poison.

Shadows creep over every surface, pulling out memories of being beaten and starved. Yet in my own way I loved the woman who brought me into this world. And now there's a little boy out there living the same exact life, from the little information that was given to me.

Something inside of my tortured and angry soul shifts as this realization dawns on me. Finn may or may not be mine. Does it really matter if he needs help? Beams of sunlight shoot through the shattered windows, lighting up the hellhole and place of torture. The rays of sunshine do their best to infuse something positive into the situation. And just like that, my question is answered.

I look back one more time before climbing into my truck and setting off. I find myself driving east to Morton, this time driving the speed limit with a clear and focused goal in my head.

I can handle the taunts and shittiness of the same assholes that live around here. I can do this because there's a little boy suffering who needs me. Jessie saved me, and now it's my turn, whether or not I'm bonded by blood. That fact never stopped Jessie or Jules from accepting me as their son. This is the something more in my life that I've craved for so damn long.

I kill the engine to my truck and walk the few blocks to the center brick elementary school building. Glancing down at my watch, I notice it's only 2:30. I lean on a telephone pole across the road from the bus lane, studying the brightly colored playground equipment. I have no idea what time school gets out but know it's soon when the canary yellow buses begin lining in front of the school.

"Shit." I run my hands through my hair.

I don't even know if kindergarten is in session. Hell, when I went to school, we only went half a day. Of course, I went to the morning session because it was the only time the school bus could pick me up, and there was no way in hell my mom would take or pick me up from school.

I study the front doors, feeling each second scrape by. It's damn torture. Part of me craves to find Ally and give her a piece of my mind. I'm afraid I'd rattle the hell out of her right now.

The front doors of the school burst open. I find myself stepping closer yet remaining a safe distance in the background. Several other parents have pulled in and leaped out of their cars, making it easy to blend in.

A whirl of bright blonde hair followed by giggles and excited chatter fills the afternoon air. A woman with her hair piled up on her head pushes up her black-framed glasses on her nose then does some chant and clap. The little line of students behind her follow and cease all chatter.

I'm not close enough to hear what the woman tells the children. I'm not even sure if she's a teacher dressed in jean capris and a baseball tee with the school logo on it. She sure in the hell doesn't look like the teachers did when I was in school. I shake the thoughts from my head and watch her crouch down and high-five each student. Some dive in for a hug while others skip by with a simple wave.

"Holy shit." I find myself taking a few steps closer when I see him.

I pinch my lips together to keep my emotions contained when I see a little boy with messy brown hair, rich chocolate eyes, and a sad smile on his face. His jeans are worn, and his tennis shoes are on their last thread. My heart constricts in my chest, and my palms go sweaty as I watch the teacher drop to her knee in front of him.

He was the last in line, I'm sure shoved to the back from the other eager students. He reaches up, wiping a stray tear from under his eyes. Kate. This has to be Kate who wraps him up in a full hug, whispering something into his ear. He nods and eventually lets go of her.

She reaches for a bag I never saw her carrying and tucks it in his backpack. An elderly woman who can barely walk makes her way over to them. Tears stream faster and hotter down Finn's face as the woman ushers him away from Kate. I remain frozen, watching my greatest nightmare play out in front of me. There are no words to explain a damn thing I'm experiencing. It's as if karma set her sights on me and won't let go.

"Max?"

I peer up to see Kate walking toward me with her hands tucked in her pockets. I open my mouth, but no words come out. When she's close enough, she extends a hand. It takes me a few moments to gather my wits and extend mine.

"Yeah," I croak out, doing my best to keep emotion void from my voice.

"I'm Kate. It's nice to meet you." She tucks her hand back in her pocket. She nibbles on her bottom lip. "I'm glad you came."

I reach back, squeezing my neck. "What do I do now?"

Kate toes her white Cons against the pavement, looking down. "I have no idea. This is my third year teaching and first year at this school. All I know is Finn needs help."

I reach out and grab Kate's hand and wait until she looks up at me. "Thank you."

Tears brim her eyes. "I don't even care if I lose my job. You know you hear about these stories in college but would never think they happen in real life, and the people here know it's going on but don't do a damn thing."

I smirk. "Yeah, you're preaching to the choir."

She tilts her head in question. I ignore it.

"Where does Ally live?"

"Miss Kate."

We both glance behind us to see a woman shading her eyes with her hand.

"You have a call on line one."

"Okay, I'll be right there." Kate turns back to me and begins backing away. "Can you meet in like forty

51

minutes over at the coffee shop on Third Avenue?"
I nod. "I'll be there."

Chapter 6

Kate

My fingers tremble as I race back into the school. He came. I really thought he wouldn't. His response was less than desirable. And after seeing the man, there's no doubt in my mind that he's Finn's dad. The phone call was from a helicopter parent and took way too long.

It was a miracle when I finally found Max's number. I was in full detective mode scouring the Internet after his parents wouldn't give it to me. I struck gold when I came across a phone number listed on an old social media account from high school. To me, it was another dead end until a deep voice answered the other line. I grab my large bag stuffed with papers and teacher manuals before racing out of my classroom.

"Shit," I hiss to myself, not remembering if I locked the door.

"Kate."

I turn to see Mr. Gilly, the principal. He's relentless, asking every Friday what my weekend plans are. He's determined to take me on a date. He's a looker, kind, and a great principal. There's no spark, and even if there was, I don't have time or intentions to date.

"Yeah." I brush back my hair and adjust my glasses on the bridge of my nose.

"Run out of contacts again?" He loosens his tie.

"Sure did." I sidestep him. "Hey, I have an appointment and am running late. Have a good weekend."

I race past him. Probably not the best thing to do, but it's past my contract time. Hell, it wouldn't matter anyway, because most nights I'm in my classroom way past dark. I have to meet Max. I'm hoping he didn't spook and run. I can't imagine what he's going through.

Not going to lie…at first, I had a gut feeling Max was just like Ally and knew he had a son but didn't give a shit. It was that first phone call that told me a different story. I can't imagine what Max is going through right now.

My clunker of a car remains in the parking lot. I can make it faster by foot to the coffee shop. I toss my bag into my car and pat my pocket, making sure my debit card is there, then I take off.

The bell above the door rings. The workers behind the counter don't look twice when I enter. I'm a normal here, typically going over curriculum and working out lesson plans. I spot Max slumped in a booth.

His thick, perfectly messy rich brown hair is

covered by a ball cap when before it was on full view. My palms grow sweaty with each step closer to him. Inhaling deeply, I move and slide right across from him in the booth.

I swear to God an older version of Finn peers up at me. The resemblance is so striking I have to force myself to focus. I tense then exhale, knowing I've said everything that needs to be said. The proverbial ball is in Max's court.

"Your normal, Kate?"

A voice startles me. I leap in the booth, the tops of my legs clanging against the bottom of the table. I spread my palms on the smooth top and inhale before nodding.

"Yes, please."

"And you?" The young barista focuses his attention on Max.

"Nothing," he growls.

I open my mouth to apologize for Max's attitude, but in all reality, there are no words.

The young man scurries off, leaving us back to our awkward silence. I clench my fingers in my free hand to keep from drumming them on the tabletop, waiting on Max to speak first.

"Thank you," he croaks out then clears his throat. "I'm not sure what the next step is."

Max opens the floodgates, and I take the invitation.

"I love Finn," I blurt out. "I had a suspicion on the first day of school. I didn't listen to the other teachers and their speculations. Finn is a bright boy. He's the smartest in his class. It was his clothes and hygiene that was my first red flag. The further I dug, the more

I became worried."

Max glances up at me prying with his stare in question, so I continue on.

"Finn had no social skills but talked easily to me. In fact, he clung to me. During our conversations, I found out he had a nana who helped raise him. It wasn't until she went to see the angels that he and his mom moved back home. Finn told me his mom wanted him to meet his real nana who lived near Morton. I've never met Ally. Finn has either ridden the bus or has been in foster care."

"Why foster care?" Max's knuckles turn white on the tabletop.

I steady my voice and continue because this man is the answer to save sweet Finn. "I reported several incidents where Finn wasn't clothed properly and showed signs of being hungry. The school ignored all of it. It wasn't until Ally's home was swept for drugs. They didn't find anything, but the cops removed Finn. The same thing has happened a few times, and that's why he's currently in foster care." The barista sets down my Chai Tea and slides a glass of ice water towards Max. I don't stop, spilling everything I've kept bottled in for months now. "I've been so damn frustrated because Child Protection Service is trained to help the parents get to a point where they can raise their children in a healthy environment, and I know there are successful stories, but it's never worked in Finn's case. It's been getting worse every time. It's like Ally has no care or even an idea she has a child. I swear whoever this Nana was raised Finn until she moved here."

"Enough." Max clenches and unclenches his fists

on the table. Without thinking, I reach over and cup his fists, soothing out the pain and agony the best I can. "He's dirty. He's hungry. The kids make fun of him I'm sure, but why was he taken this time?"

I peer down at our linked hands. "It was picture day. I bought him a nice little button-up shirt. I've been written up a couple of times for favoring Finn, but I don't care. I wanted him to feel special on picture day."

"I sent him into the bathroom off our classroom while the others were at recess to change into his shirt. Max, he came out so proud and happy of his new shirt, but the buttons were all mismatched."

I have to stop and clear my throat. My eyes sting with hurt and pain. It's a memory that I never want to live again, but I push through.

"I helped him adjust the buttons. Once I got his shirt undone and then went to fasten the buttons, that's when I saw the welts covering his chest. They were perfect triangles. When I asked him what happened, he told me his mom got super mad when her shirt fell off a hanger and hit him with it. I reported it to the school, CPS, and the cops, and that's when he was taken from Ally this last time…"

I'm not able to finish the rest of my story about being put on probation by the school board for once again overstepping boundaries before Max storms out of the booth with his jaw clenched. He glances back at me then storms off. The hurt stirring in his eyes breaks me. I whip around to see him striding right out of the door.

"Max," I holler out.

He doesn't turn around.

My chest aches for Finn and the fact his one final chance just stormed away.

Chapter 7

Max

"Your dad will appreciate that." Mom opens the truck door and snags the brown bag holding a fifth of Jack Daniels.

She damn well knows it wasn't for him or her. I wasn't thinking when I stormed into the liquor store and bought it. Drinking is something I've never fallen back on. Too damn scared to slip down that slippery slope my mom did. Today was the final straw in my game of discipline.

"Dinner is ready when you are." She waves the bag and saunters up the sidewalk.

I didn't miss the worry in her features. Jules knows not to push, and that in time, I'll crack wide open. I grab my phone out of my pocket, knowing I have a certain text to send.

Me: I'm sorry about today. I'm meeting with a lawyer in the morning.

I chew my bottom lip, not sure how to end the text. Kate has a heart of gold, and I've been nothing but an asshole to her. There's no damn handbook telling you how to act when you've been shocked with a child and one who is basically reliving your childhood. Sheer hell.

I click send, at a loss for words. The three dots at the bottom of the screen jump around, letting me know she's texting me back.

Kate: Please call if you need anything. I can keep you updated on Finn.

Me: Thanks. I appreciate it.

I know she's breaking all kinds of rules. Just goes to show what kind of person she truly is.

Dad is on the porch in his rocker and staring me down. There are two plates on the table and two drinks. I relax back in the rocker that Mom typically occupies and take a long pull of the stiff Jack Daniels drink.

"Thanks for the whiskey." He tips back his glass tumbler. "Needed one after today."

I nod. "Planned to drink the entire bottle on my own."

As hurtful as it is to open up about it, it feels damn good at the same time to admit the truth out loud, ridding that lingering demon inside of me.

"Can't say I blame ya." Dad shovels a forkful of tender roast into his mouth.

I let another harsh swallow of whiskey glide down my throat. "You know my biggest fear used to be turning out to be a drunk just like her, and now that seems so fucking ridiculous."

"Can't imagine what you're going through right now, son. All I do know is you are one of the strongest people I know, Max. You'll get through this. Focus on one step at a time. First thing is a paternity test then moving on from there."

I finish off my drink. "No need for that. He's mine, Dad. I saw him today, and there's no doubt."

He nods then slides over his drink. "I had a feeling. But still we are going to follow each step. I've already filled in the lawyer your mom and I hired. He's the best in the state, specializing in custody cases. But Max, you're going to have to keep your calm and stay patient during this process. It will be hard to do, but you're going to have to have faith."

Tears sting, but I refuse to let a single one drop. "You should've seen him. Fuck, it was a horrible vortex into time travel. He looks just like me, he was dressed in shitty clothes, and he was so damn sad when he had to leave Kate's side."

"Kate?" Dad asks, finishing off his meal.

"His kindergarten teacher. The one who called me."

"She's a damn persistent one. She called our house a dozen times, never giving up asking for your number."

"She did?" I crane my neck to look at him.

"Yeah, we chalked it up to some stalker or shit like that."

"I wonder how she got my number?" I whisper to myself. The setting sun catches my question in its crisp air. All I do know is I'm so damn thankful she

61

did.

Chapter 8

Kate

It's been two weeks and not one word from Max. It's as if he disappeared off the face of the world. I get that it may be too much for him, but Finn needs him. My hands have been tied after being written up and put on probation by the school board. Someone reported seeing Max and me together at the local coffee shop.

It's all bullshit, and I know it. It's a good old small town, and all of its politics it keeps locked away in the depths, the narrow-minded school board members doing their best to brush everything under the carpet. They have no intention of helping Finn. Instead, they are more worried about looking good from the street.

My phone pings in my pocket. I pull it out to see a text from Mr. Gilly. Steven is relentless in his efforts. His actions become less subtle each time I turn him down. He claims he's on my side and he couldn't help me with being written up. It's all bullshit, and the longer time goes on, the more livid I become.

Gilly: Just checking in on you. I have an extra ticket to the movies if you want to join me.

I ignore it, but before I can tuck my phone away into my pocket and go back to scanning the shelves of the local hardware store, the tiny bubbles begin popping up and down.

Gilly: And dinner of course.

It's the final nail in his coffin. I'm fed up with his attempts and no action when it comes to doing the right thing. The letter on my computer to the state Board of Education will be sent tomorrow.

Me: No.

Me: Actually, I'd appreciate if you'd quit asking me out. It's never going to happen. I have no interest. And this is quickly approaching harassment.

The bubbles dance again, but I'm faster this time, powering off my phone and putting it back in my pocket. I glance back to the shelf, scanning for the can of Gloss Ocean Blue spray paint. I scored three chairs at a yard sale and ran out of paint. A smile graces my face, knowing my students will love their new reading chairs.

"Shit," I hiss to myself, spotting it on the top shelf and way to the back. "Are you serious?"

I glance around seeing a five-gallon bucket with a lid and grab it. Not the smartest idea, but right now my patience has run thin, and I know it will take forever for Old Man Pete to help me. He moves about as fast as thick tar and will want to talk for thirty minutes about the weather.

I snag the bucket and place it right in front of the wall of spray paint. I test it out and make sure it's sturdy enough. Even with the extra height from standing on the bucket, I'm still forced to go up on the tips of my toes. I grab a can of another color, reaching with everything I have to scoot the damn blue my way.

Right when my fingers wrap around the top of the can, the bucket pitches, sending me forward into the shelves. My hand gets caught between an open space in the shelf and doesn't give.

"Shit," I hiss out, cringing in pain as something in my wrist pops and I sail towards the harsh tile floor.

It never comes. Instead, I'm wrapped in strong arms.

"Not a smart idea, Kate." A voice vibrates against my neck.

The pain throbbing in my wrist dulls as Max's scent wraps me in a gentle hug. I open my mouth to speak, but no words come out. He sets me on the ground, and I adjust my shirt down around my middle. Max extends his hand out toward me.

"Is this what you were going for?"

I nod. Not only did he catch me from a major crash, but also managed to grab the can of spray paint. I reach out to grab it and wince in pain, unable to hold it.

"Jesus, Kate, your wrist." Max grabs my upper arm, bringing it closer to him.

I realize it's already swollen at least double in size.

"It got caught," I squeak out.

"You probably broke it." He begins guiding me to the front. There's a harshness in his tone that makes me stop and stiffen my spine.

"I'm fine." I pull back.

"Bullshit. You need to go to the hospital now." He begins walking again. "Pete, put this on my account."

I'm outside and being lifted into Max's truck. He jogs around the front of it. I can't help but notice the resemblance to Finn, even in their simple gestures. His jaw is clenched as he fires up the truck and backs out of the local hardware store parking lot.

"You don't have to do this. It's clear you're not impressed." I turn to him. "Just let me out. I can drive one-handed."

The pain doesn't even register with the mystery of this man sitting next to me. Talk about one screwed-up puzzle.

"You're right." He glances over at me, searing me with those rich chocolate eyes. "I'm not impressed. I'm pissed off."

"You're an ass. Let me out," I demand again.

He chuckles. The man actually has the nerve to laugh right now.

"I take that back. You're a major asshole."

He shakes his head as he turns into the small hospital. Nothing like living in a small town where everything is located on the main road. He kills the engine and turns toward me, piercing me with his damn good looks.

"I'm pissed over the fact you couldn't ask for help." He reaches over and squeezes the top of my thigh. "I can't stand seeing people in pain or hurt."

And with that, he's out of the truck and making his way to my side. He's all gentleman opening the door for me and ushering me inside. I don't get a chance to speak at all. Max takes it upon himself to get me checked in. There's a presence about him that no one can deny. I don't miss the way the young nurse drinks him in. And just like that, I find myself in an emergency room.

Once Samantha, the overly flirty nurse, leaves the room, the silence is thick, threatening to smother me. The throbbing pain in my wrist begins to radiate up my arm. The patience that was running thin before has now blown. I rip off the Band-Aid.

"Finn goes back to his mom next week." I stare him down. "CPS has claimed her reformed and capable of caring for him. It's bullshit."

Max doesn't say a word, so I take it upon myself to push forward.

"He's been doing so well with this set of foster parents. It's going to break my heart when it happens. I swear, why doesn't she just give him away? And why in the hell are you back here? I thought you left, fleeing from your problems and not facing them just like everyone else in Finn's life."

My rant is cut off when the door to the stale room opens.

"Hi, Miss Valent…"

"Yes, that's me." I wave from the table, the paper crunching underneath me, saving the man from butchering my last name.

"I'm here to take you for x-rays." The gentle giant approaches me. "Any chance you're pregnant or could be?"

I snort then burst into laughter. I slap my hand over my mouth. My sex life is non-existent and has been since forever. Yeah, I'm that girl who is okay dying a sex-starved woman, just not an old cat lady.

"I'll take that as a no," he responds.

I'm ushered down a long hall then go through the process of getting my arm x-rayed. I stay quiet through it all but learn everything about Hank, from how he married his high school sweetheart to the names of his six dogs.

"The doctor will be in shortly. You want some more ice for your wrist?" Hank asks.

"No, thanks."

"Yes, she does." Max kicks his legs out in front of him.

"All righty then. I'll be right back."

"Ass," I mumble as Hank closes the door.

"Thought I was a major asshole." Max crooks up a smile, putting his perfect, white teeth on display, making me angrier that I find him so damn good looking.

"You are, and quit treating me like a damn child."

I scoot back on the table as Max stands to full height and stretches his arms over his head. I keep my focus on the watercolor painting on the wall and not his torso.

"I'm a concerned friend. If I'm treating you like a

child, I'm sorry. I played football for years and know ice is crucial to help with swelling."

Hank walks back in and hands the ice to Max, who takes it upon himself to walk over to me and place it on my wrist.

"And to answer your question, I'm back here because I now live here."

I whip my head his direction, my jaw slack in shock. "You what?"

Max places his hand on the top of my thigh. The heat from his skin burns me from the inside. "I grew up in Boone. Went home that day to my parents' house and made a plan."

"I thought you left," I whisper.

"Yeah, I was sensing that from your attitude toward me."

Max goes on to fill me in on the fact he hired a lawyer and is remodeling a house. He makes it clear he's not about to share the entire process with me. From college and studying the law on my own, I know it's going to be a daunting procedure with lots of hoops to jump through. We are cut off when a young and very good-looking doctor steps in. And I mean this man could take out McDreamy from Grey's easily.

"Kate Wilson-Valentukonis, I'm Doctor Ash." He extends his hand. Mine trembles in his large one. "I see you had an accident."

"Yeah," I stutter out. "You actually pronounced my last name right. That's rare."

Max steps back, taking his seat and giving the handsome doctor some room.

"Well, the x-ray shows a hairline fracture." He

points it out on the picture. "We are going to have to wait for the swelling to go down before we can cast it."

I groan. "Not a cast. I don't have time for that."

"Shouldn't have been standing on a damn bucket then," Max adds from the corner.

"Yeah, your boyfriend is right," Doctor Ash says as he places a metal piece under my hand and begins wrapping it with a bandage.

"He's not my boyfriend."

"Really?" Ash freezes and looks at me, shooting up an eyebrow.

"I'm her fiancé." Max stands, taking my side.

"Well, congratulations. Good thing you weren't wearing your ring. We may have had to cut it off."

My cheeks burn with fiery flames of embarrassment. This day can't get over soon enough.

"I'll write a script for pain pills." Dr. Hot Pants goes on about care, then gives us our goodbyes.

As soon as the door shuts, I hop off the table and shoot daggers at Max. "What was that about?"

"He was hitting on you. I'm no fool, Kate."

"And so what if he was?" I strike back.

"It's unprofessional as hell." He shrugs.

"God, you're irritating."

Chapter 9

Max

"So you're just going to hold me hostage?" Kate glares at me as I climb back in the truck.

Even though she refused to have the pain meds filled, I did it anyway. Grabbed two bottles of wine, a frozen pizza, and a bag of salad.

"I know you said you'd nurse your wound with wine, so I had to take a stab at what kind."

"What did you get?" She peeks in the bag.

"Moscato."

"Perfect. That's my favorite."

Kate hitches a thumb over her shoulder to all of the shit in the bed of my truck. "Looks more like you're building a house, not remodeling one."

"It was in horrible shape."

"This is weird. Just take me back to my car," Kate blurts out.

"I'm going to feed you and make sure the pain doesn't get too bad. There's no getting out of it."

Yeah, I can play up that card, but the fact is I want to be around this woman. She's gorgeous with long, toned legs, messy blonde hair, and freckles that sprinkle the top of her exposed shoulder. Her feisty attitude intrigues me, and at this point, I owe her everything.

"Why are we going to Cody's Shaggin' Shack?" Kate's face turns a shade of green. It's damn adorable. She rights her glasses on the bridge of her nose.

"Been trashed on the Pussy Pleaser before?" I guess.

"One time." She holds up a finger. "And I've never been back. That Cody is the devil disguised in clothes behind a bar and sure knows how to sling drinks. He kept them coming all night long."

I chuckle. "Yeah, I've heard plenty of those stories."

I pull in beside the bar, continuing down the lane. "Cody is one of my mom and dad's best friends. They went to high school together. He moved here after high school and opened the bar. He has a house that needs work and offered it to me when he heard of my situation."

"Oh." She nods her head.

"I'm warning you, it's still pretty rough on the inside."

"It's cute," Kate replies, taking in the small farmhouse.

"I'll get that," I say when she grabs a grocery bag. Her stubbornness shines through.

"I have a fractured wrist. You act like my leg was sawed off." Her grip tightens on the bags.

"You're stubborn as hell, woman," I grumble.

"And you're pushy as hell, so get over it." She pokes out her tongue.

"Real mature," I grumble and go about packing the supplies to a safe place.

Not only does Kate help pack in the groceries, I find her rolling pale yellow paint on the walls of the bathroom. I lean on the doorjamb, taking her in as she hums a familiar tune. Her tongue pokes out to the side as she concentrates. I packed the supplies into the shed, which took a whopping fifteen minutes, max. This woman.

"Are you just gonna stare or help?" Kate asks, keeping her attention on the wall.

"Think I'll just stare."

She glances over her shoulder. "Not a fan of painting?"

"Despise it. Mom and my little sister have done all the painting up to this point."

"You know how to run an oven?"

I shrug, battling the playful smile fighting to come out. It's a foreign feeling. I have no idea how long it's been since a genuine and carefree one came my way.

"Figure it out, because that bottle of wine has my name on it after the day I've had." Kate stretches, rolling the paint along the wall and giving me a glimpse of her toned skin. I bite back a growl. This woman has done something to me. It's more than the fact she's brought my world full circle. It's her honest and carefree nature that's driven to protect the innocent and right all the wrongs in the world. If I've learned anything in the small amount of time on this

73

earth, it's that there are very few who protect the underdogs.

"Got it, teach." I wink and push off the doorjamb.

She rolls her eyes at my stupid nickname. I'd give anything to stay in place razzing the hell out of her. The fact is her wrist will begin throbbing any minute. She's high on adrenaline, and the pain will settle in with a punch to the gut. Quite frankly, I don't give a shit if she eases that ache with the bottles of wine or a few pills. I just know she doesn't deserve the pain.

I pop the pizzas into the oven even though it's not pre-heated. The bag of shredded cheese lies on the counter, waiting to top the hot goodness of the pizza. I take in my surroundings for the thousandth time, wondering if Finn will ever enter these doors. From what my lawyer has told me, it's going to be a bit of an uphill battle for me. Courts don't like taking children away from their moms; however, in Ally's case, she's sealed her own fate. Time and going through all the steps is what it's going to take. The one thing I know is I won't give up.

The buzzer goes off. I turn to the oven, wondering where in the hell the last fifteen minutes went. At the same time, Kate rounds the corner, wringing her hands with a dry towel.

I give her a nod, then force myself to focus on taking out the pizza. It's not a golden brown, so I sprinkle the extra cheese on and put it back on the rack, setting the timer for four minutes.

"This place is pretty damn cool." Kate grabs a plastic cup from the cupboard and twists off the top of the wine.

I relax back on the counter, thanking the gods

above I decided to buy two smaller bottles with twist-off tops versus the larger bottle with a cork. Kate continues pouring an ample amount of wine into a plastic cup.

"It's really cute, Max. Perfect for you and Finn. I swear I can see him sitting at that table doing his homework." She brings the cheap plastic blue cup to her lips, taking a sip.

"It's not done." I admit my biggest fear.

Kate doesn't respond, only tilting her head to the side in question.

"The DNA test has been done against my will. I knew he was mine the moment I saw him. Some legality shit or something. I'm his father and now my lawyer is serving papers and following all the ropes to get me in Finn's life. I sure in the hell hope he thrives in this house one day."

"Max." Kate sits down her plastic cup, her full lips parted, but the timer to the oven interrupts her thoughts.

I bend down, pulling out the perfect pizza, and set it on the make-shift island. One day it will be a creation made from my hands out of the old barn wood from Mom and Dad's farm. All in time.

"Hope you like Hawaiian pizza." I hate this shit but figured the odds were if I despise it, Kate may like it. I slice it into eighths and serve her a few pieces on a paper plate, then tear open the bag of salad and open the bottle of ranch.

Kate doesn't hesitate preparing her plate. I stand back watching her drizzle the dressing all over the pizza. Just like Whit. I pick the piece with the least amount of pineapple and plan to pick off all the vile pieces from my slices. It's then I see Kate plucking the fruit from her pizza.

It seems we catch each other at the same time, then erupt into a battle of laughter. From there on, we eat the cheese, salad, and crust, forgoing the damn sweet juice of fruit. Kate pours herself another glass of wine as I pop open a bottle of beer.

We chat about everything and sip our drinks in the moments of silence. I keep an eye on Kate's broken wrist. I swear, watching her go down in that tiny hardware store brought back way too many memories, the ones I've fought to forget since being honorably discharged.

I never had a family I left behind, or at least I thought so. I guess the joke was on me. I spent months agonizing over the fact my brothers went home in body bags. Their children would never know them, when all the time I didn't know I had one waiting for me. Not only waiting, but enduring the same pain I did as a child.

Kate finishes off her second cup of wine then covers her mouth. "I need to use the restroom."

I nod. "You know where it is."

I can't help myself, watching her tight little ass sway as she walks away from the island. Her golden locks swing back and forth, hypnotizing me and making a part of me stir to life. It's not the same as porno mags or videos; Kate is so much damn more. I have no idea how to explain it.

When Kate's hypnotic vibes evaporate, I go about cleaning up the kitchen, washing the pan I baked the pizza on, and tossing our plates in the trash. I fill her cup of wine and grab another bottle of beer for me.

When she doesn't reappear in a decent amount of time, I go to look for her. The bathroom door remains cracked open.

Kate's not in there. It doesn't take me long to figure out where she is as the ray of light from my bedroom blinds me. I waltz in with my beer securely in one hand and her wine in the other. Kate's figure illuminates in front of my used dresser, a thin piece of paper held before her face.

I don't have to ask what she's looking at. It's me and Finn's mom. My first love. The woman I would've laid everything down for. I'm not sure if it's the alcohol or the exhaustion from the last two weeks, but I walk right up behind her, placing the cup of wine on the top of the worn dresser.

My free hand roams down to her waist, gripping it tightly. My front presses to her backside as she continues to study the picture. With her free hand, she grabs the cup of wine, bringing it to her lips. The tension between us is so damn hot it sears my flesh, and I can't figure out why.

Once she sets the cup down on the dresser and glances back at the picture, her focus is again back on my "happily ever after." I tilt my beer back, letting the liquid numb my senses just enough to ask the next question about to escape my lips.

"Tell me about him."

"She's so beautiful here. I swear I barely recognize her."

My grip on her hips digs into her flesh.

"Tell me about him."

"He dips everything into ketchup." Kate relaxes back into me.

I remain silent, tilting my beer back again. My body is exhausted from transforming this junkyard into something that resembles a home.

"Finn hates vegetables. He's smarter than any of his peers. He can do fifth grade math. He loves routine, and when that's broken, he's devastated."

Kate reaches for her wine, taking another long gulp. "He hates sports and is all brain. He loves school and building things with his hands. Finn is so damn brilliant, and if he had the right environment, I swear he'd be the next Einstein. Life beats him down, but he never gives up."

I'm forced to tip back my beer because Kate has no damn idea how close she just hit to home.

"Keep telling me," I murmur into her sweet, honey nectar flesh.

"Like I said, Finn loves ketchup. It doesn't matter if it's meat or fruit, he has to have that one constant." Kate's wounded wrist cascades down to my side, and her body goes limp. "I'm so tired."

"He sounds perfect." I keep her body in my arms as she melts into me. "Kate, I'll never be man enough to thank you. There's just nothing I could do to ever show you how thankful I am."

Her sweet and perfect body grows even heavier from exhaustion. I carry her to the mattress and tug my favorite blankets to her chin. Seeing her perfect and innocent silhouette in my bed undoes me.

Her eyes flutter once, then twice, before she loses the battle and succumbs to sleep. I'd love nothing more than to cuddle the shit out of this woman until she doesn't feel any more pain in her arm. I'd give her anything because she just gave me the world and doesn't even know it.

It takes force to walk away from her. In due time, I do walk away and collapse on the couch. I never once thought in my life I could endure more pain than I already have. Life had nothing on me, or that's what I thought until I closed my eyes and saw the spitting image of me at that age. It's the sweet innocence of Kate's smile and wild blonde hair that breaks through the nightmare. It's a foreign feeling that I crave and fear at the same time. She has my head all sorts of messed up.

Chapter 10

Kate

It was cheap white wine. And it was sweet as hell. Then I woke up wrapped in Max's scent. It was perfect and lonely as hell because he wasn't there. My wrist ached and my head throbbed. I remembered glimpses of the night before. Me painting, pizza, wine, and Max. Then the rest dulled to life as I forced myself out of Max's bed.

"Kate, you don't need your insurance. Max took care of it."

I blink once, then twice.

"Excuse me?"

"The young gentleman who came in with you paid your bill last night."

"Okay." I step back into the waiting room, staying for the on-call doctor to see if see my arm is ready to cast.

The room spins a bit as I absorb the news the receptionist just told me. I don't even remember Max pulling out his wallet. I woke up in his bed, and he was gone. The wine really hit me hard. Honestly, I'm not sure it was entirely the wine that made my knees go lax and my entire body go limp. I have no doubt it was Max's woodsy scent and body pressed up against my back.

And I'm not about to admit how my heart fluttered in disappointment to find the bed empty and yellow note on the lone pillow. He left a quick message in his blocky, masculine print, letting me know he left his truck keys for me since he had to go out of town to get a load of siding, that he'd have Cody take him to his truck later this afternoon, and to leave the keys in the toolbox. He also said he left a plate of breakfast for me in the microwave.

I was expecting Toaster Strudels or something. I couldn't have been more off base; I opened the door and came eye to eye with a plate of bacon, hash browns, and eggs.

I have no idea how long I sit in the hospital waiting room before my name is called. Then while the doctor wraps my arm in plaster, I berate myself internally for not asking more questions about Finn and what Max is planning to do. It's very straightforward, but then again, not a subject I'm willing to let go easily.

"Kate, you're set to go." Doctor Ash pats my shoulder.

His sex appeal and charm do nothing for me. Any other time in my life, I'd be all over this opportunity, especially living in a small town and being single. There's not a very big pond and even fewer fish. It's Max who controls my thoughts, from his mysterious parts to his good looks.

Doctor Ash begins to speak. "This goes against all kinds of ethics, but if you ever want to grab dinner, I'm available."

He's right. It's not the right place. Dinner with a hot guy who is a doctor is a no-brainer. I muster up some shred of wanting, but nothing ever comes.

I push my glasses up on the bridge of my nose and slide off the table. "Thank you, but I don't really have time to date."

I cringe. Visibly cringe from my own string of stupid words. He said nothing about dating, but leave it up to me to make this awkward. I need coffee and a hot shower to wash away this fog that lingers over me.

He nods and steps back, raising an eyebrow. "Well, if you ever find the time, Kate Wilson-Valentukonis, you know where to find me."

Damn, the way my name sounds being perfectly pronounced, rolling off his tongue, is damn hot even though I'm not interested. The pain in my wrist is still a dull ache. The clunky cast is already a pain in the ass on my drive home. I take a longing glance at Cody's bar as I drive past it. I didn't admit to Max that I live only a few blocks from him in an old farmhouse. The rent is cheap because the owner passed away, and the children didn't want to sell a piece of their heritage. They were looking for someone to live in it and take care of it.

It's truly not a hardship. The two-story house, which is way too much for me, is bordered by a pristine white picket fence. It's simple elegance.

"Of course, I'd have to break my right wrist." I

blow my bangs out of my face struggling to get in the door.

I growl in frustration as it dawns on me that taking a relaxing shower isn't going to be so damn easy. It's moments like these I want my momma. Being the only child, I was always doted on and taken care of. My loving parents are now traveling the world and loving their lifestyle. They deserve it after having me so late in life.

After studying the shower for several minutes, I give up on the idea for now. I open the bottle of pain pills I refused to take last night and pop one in. Soon the world grows hazy and I'm sinking onto my couch, pulling my favorite quilt on top of me. It's Max's scent, strong jawline, and piercing eyes that fill my senses before sleep takes over.

***

This is the dumbest idea ever. I'm about to turn around when I get a glimpse of Max's backside. He's shirtless, heaving large, long boxes off a flatbed trailer. I stand frozen with the plate of cookies in my hands. My jaw slackens at the sight of layers of muscle rippling with each of his movements.

It's not hot outside by any means, but I find myself heating up from head to toe underneath my leggings and baggy sweater. Sweat droplets drip down his back, but it's when he turns to face me that I too begin to sweat.

A dazzling smile lights up his face as he strides toward me. "Nice gear."

He nods to the lime green cast on my right hand.

I shrug and extend the plate toward him, thanking God I brought them with me because it would have taken all of my will not to leap into his hard, chiseled chest.

"Here. A thank you."

Max takes the plate of cookies wrapped in Saran Wrap. "What's this for?" He quirks an eyebrow.

"A thank you for taking care of me last night, making me breakfast, and paying my bill." I reach down into my pocket, tug out the bundle of money, and extend it his way.

"The hell? You push drugs too or something?" He lifts the wrap, not waiting to taste the cookies.

I snort in laughter. Not lady-like at all. "No, broke into my piggy bank."

"I'm not taking it." He shoves a cookie in his mouth, taking a large bite. Crumbs linger on his mouth. I bite down on my bottom lip, stifling the moan building up inside of me. What has this man done to me?

"Why not? Pretty darn sure that wasn't a little bill and it was no fault of yours." I take a step back as Max finishes his second cookie.

"Kate, just gonna say it one time. And as screwed up as it may sound, it's how I feel. There's no way in hell I'll ever be able to pay you back." He holds up a hand. "And before your smart mouth goes off about not needing to be paid back, listen to me. The thought of me living the rest of my life not knowing I had a son out there guts me. Not to mention the thoughts of the abuse he's suffered at the hands of a disgusting human being more obsessed with drugs and getting her next fix."

"But…" I try.

"You are hard-headed as hell with a stubborn streak to match, Kate. I'm not hearing any of it, and thanks for the home-baked cookies. I'm a sucker for sweets." He nods to the porch. "Want a drink? I need a break."

"Sure," I squeak out, clasping my fingers together as we walk to the small porch framing the house. The fresh boards lining the floor and the railing let me know the porch must have been the first thing Max worked on.

"This is nice. I didn't notice it last night." I run my hand along the railing.

"Thanks. I'll be right back." He points to one of the rocking chairs and then disappears into the house.

Rattling of glasses fills the air as I continue to run my hand down the railing and finally take a seat in a rocking chair. The screen door swings open, revealing Max holding two copper mugs while chowing down on another cookie.

"You like Moscow Mules?" He sets them both down on the table between us.

I shrug. It seems it's the only thing I know how to do. "Never had one."

"Then you'll love them. It's my specialty." He winks.

"This porch is amazing," I admit, picking up my mug.

"My dad said a porch makes the house, so it was the first thing I worked on."

I bring the copper mug to my lips, taking a tiny sip. "Mmmm. That's tasty and refreshing. Thanks."

He rests his head back on the rocker, his neck fully

exposed as he takes a drink. "You ever been afraid of something so bad that you keep it around yourself so it doesn't haunt you?"

His deep question throws me for a loop. Silence floats between us before I internalize his question.

"Not sure what you're talking about, Max." I twist in my chair, tucking a leg underneath me in order to face him.

"My birth mom was an alcoholic. She drank herself to death and managed to beat the hell out of me on the way." He pauses briefly, rubbing small scars on his chest. "The first day I saw Finn and talked to you, I went to the liquor store and bought a bottle. Planned to drink the whole son of a bitch then buy another, but it was my dad who stopped me. He grabbed the bottle and poured me a drink. We shared a few, and I knew then I was stronger than the demon I could so easily fall into."

"I'm sorry, Max."

He goes on, telling me everything about his past and his mother and how Jessie, his football coach, saved him and took him in. My heart aches with each word that flows from Max's lips.

"And now I'm about to get custody of my own son, saving him from the same life I lived, and how the hell do I know I'm going to be any better than what he's coming from?"

Without thinking, I reach over and grab his hand. "I get it now. You hold that pain close and let it go slowly. Max, I barely know you but can already tell you're going to be one hell of a dad. So many men would've driven out of town and never looked back."

He nods. "I get to meet him on Wednesday. It's

going to be supervised. My lawyer is pushing for full custody. The shitty thing is the system protects Ally's rights as long as she's showing progress. At the moment, she's not, but I don't trust her not to. I can only hope she gives up all rights to him."

A bubble of happiness and nerves blooms inside of me. I can see the light at the end of the tunnel. It's finally time for someone to stand up for Finn. I remain speechless for several moments not knowing what in the hell to say.

"I'm so proud of you, Max."

"I have lots of work to do before Wednesday to get this place in shape. The visit is going to be here."

I hop up from the rocker, my head spinning a bit from the sudden movement. "Let's get going then."

Max stands up, grabbing the last cookie from the plate.

"You are like a garbage disposal," I say, taking a step closer to him.

A crooked smile lights up his face. "The Sprinkles Bakery chocolate chip cookies are my favorite. My true weakness."

"You jerk." I slap his chest. "How come…"

He grabs my hand, tugging me toward him. "I thought I'd let you indulge in a little white lie."

"And he has jokes on top of his good looks and heart." I shake my head.

Max drops his hands to my hips, tugging me to him until we are chest to chest. I splay my palms out on his chest. My fingertips sear to life with the contact.

"You think I'm cute. Is that what you're saying?"

He tilts his head, bringing a hand up to my cheek."

"You know you are, Max," I whisper.

He runs the pad of his thumb over my cheek. "You're not half bad yourself."

A shrieking voice pulls us out of our trance. We were seconds from brushing our lips together.

"Max!" I turn to see a teenage girl running our way. She halts in her tracks as soon as she puts together the scene.

And then it's like an army of people follow her, all decked out in work clothes. Some carry coolers while others pack supplies.

"Whit." Max jerks his chin and takes a step back, but before he does, he whispers in my ear, causing flutters to ignite low in my belly. "It's my family. They are tough as hell when it comes to me but mean well. Hang tight. You're about to get the full meal deal with us."

"Okay," I whisper.

And just like that, Max's family, along with Cody, invade our moment of peace. Paint brushes fly, hammers swing, and we all work in unison.

"Max hates painting. I find it so soothing." His mom peers over her shoulder with a gentle smile.

"I agree. I love painting. Guess that's why I always wanted to teach kindergarten."

The humor in my words fall flat. I don't miss the side eye glares that Whit, Max's little sister, keeps sending my way. She snorts but doesn't say a word as she continues to run the roller on the wall.

"Whit, why don't you go see if your dad needs help?" Jules suggests.

"Whatever." She rolls her eyes and stomps off.

"You're a smart girl for picking a grade to teach when they're cute and lovable compared to the hell days of puberty and teenagers."

I drop my roller in the pan and sit down on a bucket. His dad was stand-offish while his other siblings flocked to Max. Jules has been friendly but tentative, and all of a sudden I feel like an enemy on traitor lines.

"I met Max because of Finn. That's it."

"Oh honey," Jules pats my shoulder, "it's nothing personal. We are all protective of Max. He's been through hell, and it's our job to protect him. I'll admit, we may go overboard sometimes."

"I'm not a bad person." The words are out of my mouth before I can take them back.

Jules kneels down before me. "Then prove it to us. Max is pretty damn quiet and keeps to himself since serving his country. If I was a betting person, I'd put all my chips on the fact he likes you a lot."

And with that she goes right back to painting and humming to herself.

Chapter 11

Max

"You walked here?" I ask.

She nods. "I only live a few blocks away."

"Then I'm walking you home." I grab her hand, leaving no room for argument.

Kate worked her ass off on Sunday, not letting her cast get in the way. She took my family's judgmental analysis like a champ. It took me having a side conversation with Whit to get her damn hackles down. I had to remind her it was because of Kate that we found out about Finn.

Kate came back on Monday after school and today, not asking how she could help. Instead she jumped right in, doing what needed to be done. That fact alone relieved me, because I was at the point of being so overwhelmed, I had no idea where to even start.

I had a sports-themed room all set up for Finn right down to the wallpaper border. The paint for the walls was, of course, my college colors, along with framed posters of my football players. It was with a gentle ease that Kate pointed out Finn despises sports.

Then the magic happened. She didn't waste one thing I bought and only had to run to the store for chalkboard paint. The walls are the same colors I planned but now have a chalkboard border for Finn to work out math problems. She brought in live plants he can tend, abstract art, and a minimal number of toys. The room is crisp and clean and not overwhelming at all. She reassures me it's an area where Finn will feel safe and comfortable, and I trust her.

The football pictures ended up in my bedroom, and the rest of the stuff I had no problem donating to the local second-hand store.

"It's fine." Kate swings our connected hands.

I glance down to our connection. "I know it's fine if I walk you home."

"You know what I mean." She rolls her eyes, her cheeks flushing the slightest hue of delicate pink.

We haven't had another moment like we had on the porch. It's been nothing but busting our asses for tomorrow. There hasn't been one second go by that I don't find myself wondering how she would've tasted and felt against me.

"How about we detour over a few blocks and share a pizza?" I squeeze her hand in mine.

Kate freezes in front of a stop sign, looking up at me. She nibbles on her lower lip, which I've picked up is her tell-tale sign. I give her the time she needs to spill what has her all bothered.

"Um, would you mind grabbing the pizza and coming back to my house?"

I shake my head side to side. "Not at all, but gonna need to know why, babe."

Kate remains silent. I can see each of her thoughts play out on her features as she decides whether to tell me or not. The setting sun cascades over, arranging the scene perfectly. That almost forgotten kiss comes crashing back in. I lean closer, feeling Kate's chest rise and fall against mine. The moment consumes me.

"I'm going to kiss you, Kate." I run my lips along hers.

She doesn't say a word. Instead she leans forward, fueling the desire low in my core. I drop a hand down to her hip, tugging her closer, and cup her cheek with my other. I move slow, relishing each second of this sweet miracle. Something inside me tells me I'll never be able to get enough of this woman.

I glide my lips across hers, unable to stifle the moan. It rolls out, vibrating off our lips. Kate takes me by surprise when she leads the kiss, her magical lips sealing to mine. She tilts her head, allowing me to deepen our connection. She's sinful, tender, and all too consuming. I sweep my tongue in her mouth. She follows suit. We kiss for what seems like forever and no time at all. When a semi-truck's Jake brakes sound around us, we break apart.

I brush the pad of my thumb over her plump, full bottom lip. "And to think that was just our first kiss."

"I've never been kissed like that." She ducks her head down.

Using my fingers under her chin, I tilt her face

back to me. "No need to be shy, and now you can explain about me getting the pizza."

She twists her lips side to side after releasing the plump lower one from her teeth. "My principal is a dick. He's been riding me about having a relationship with you."

Rage consumes me but doesn't overpower me. Her beauty and the glow from the sleepy sun trumps it all.

"He's asked me out several times, and right before I broke my arm, I sent him a text basically telling him off, and he wasn't so kind to me yesterday and today at school."

I step closer, tugging her to me. "What did he do?"

I can't help the growl that escapes me. The thought of some power-hungry douche bag treating her like shit makes me see red. Intimidation and bullying are a hard limit for me, no matter who is involved.

I get he's more than likely enamored by Kate. Who in the hell wouldn't be? And I haven't seen her in action in the classroom but have no reservation that she's one hell of a teacher. I know this without a shadow of doubt by the way she talks about her students and the hours she puts into planning her lessons, not to mention the money she spends on her classroom. I've learned all this in just the few days I've been around Kate. It's her passion.

"It's embarrassing." She drops her head to my chest, avoiding eye contact.

"Kate." I urge her on.

"He pulled me in his office." Her voice is muffled by my chest. It takes everything inside me not to force her to look up at me. "He wrote me up and said when it happens again, I'll be put on a plan."

"What in the hell did he write you up for?" This time I don't dare to hide the fierceness of my growl.

"I forgot to turn in my lesson plans on Friday. He caught me this morning putting them in his box. It was the first time I was late with them. He's just pissed I turned him down."

I step back, placing my hands on her shoulders and waiting for her to face me. When she does, tears swim in her gorgeous eyes. Not on my damn watch.

"You go to the superintendent, and if he doesn't listen, then you go to the school board. This is bullshit and straight-up wrong." As soon as the words are out of my mouth, I tug her back to me. "There's no negotiating on this topic."

"It's a small town, Max. They can do whatever they want."

"You're preaching to the choir, babe. But you will stand up for yourself." I kiss the top of her head. "You're gonna have to let me go, so I can get us dinner."

Her tender giggle puts a smile on my face. "You're the one squeezing me to death."

"Lies, all lies." I kiss the top of her hand before stepping back. "What's your address?"

She fires it off as I walk backward, running my hands through my unruly hair to keep myself from grabbing her sweet-ass body again. I turn around, knowing damn well I have to or we won't be eating anything tonight. Or at least, I will be and it won't be pizza.

"No pineapple." A voice echoes down the road as

I jog across the crosswalk.

I glance back to barely see Kate with her hands cupped around her mouth.

"Got it. Extra pineapple."

"No."

A genuine spark of laughter vibrates from deep in my chest. I'm so screwed with this woman.

The pizza joint is packed. We should've called in our order. I haven't eaten here yet. Not very proud of it, but I've been pretty much living off bar food from Cody's. Damn lucky he's open late. I've been busting my ass remodeling the house. It's been damn long days and nights working with my hands while keeping up with my business of designing and managing websites at night.

I keep my head down as I make my way to the counter. Besides Deputy Dickhead, I haven't run into anyone else from my past. It's a damn miracle. Even though we are a good fifteen miles from Boone doesn't mean shit doesn't mesh, and news travels fast. I'm guessing things are going to heat up after Ally is served papers.

"How can I help you?" a young teenager asks from behind the counter.

The menu is overwhelming as hell. Calzones, pizza, salads of every kind you could think of.

"You have a special?" I ask.

"Two large pizzas for twenty-five dollars, which includes a two-liter of soda."

That's no damn help. I gaze up at the menu and take a wild guess.

"I'll take that. One pepperoni and make the other one a Sour Pig." I tug my wallet out of my back pocket.

As I'm paying the tab, I'm pretty sure there was no way I went wrong. Everyone loves pepperoni, and I'm a damn sucker for sauerkraut. The combination of it on pizza is perfection. Reminds me of the days I served and the dozens of pizzas my buddy and I would wolf down.

I relax back on an exposed beam, waiting on my order. I find myself enjoying the memories of serving, without being haunted by them. I traveled the world, made lifelong bonds, and served my country. It's just what I needed to soothe the longing lingering in my soul. It's something I'll never regret, even if I did miss out on Finn's life. It's taken me a while to digest that everything happens for a reason. Ally's poison, and even if I didn't serve, she never would've told me about Finn. Who knows if I'd have crossed paths with Kate? None of it adds up. All I do know is I'm glad I'm standing right where I am.

A loud ruckus gets my attention. Turning, I see a table of ghosts from the past. Ironic since seconds ago I was thankful I hadn't run into anyone I knew. Deputy Dickhead is flanked with all his friends from high school. I recognize most of them but don't take long glancing their way. I'm thankful as fuck the joint is jam-packed and the odds of them seeing me are slim.

Steven Gilly, Cole's sidekick back in the day, sits on the end. Steven was never quite as popular or near the athlete Cole was. I turn my head and smirk, thinking how damn funny life is. I'm in better shape than any of those pukes. But Steven has aged far better than Cole. Wonder what Steven is up to? He may be Deputy Dingleberry.

I focus on the orders being slinged out. I can't remember if I gave them my name or not.

"You tap that ass you've been eyeing yet?" Cole's voice floats over the restaurant. There's some razzing then riotous laughter echoing around the room.

"Sir, here's your order."

I move before the employee has a chance to set the two boxes on the counter and get the hell out of there. The walk is quick and brisk to Kate's house. I follow the street signs and don't even need to glance up to the number on her house to know it's hers. The quaint white fence and adorable house is so her. I swing open the gate and step in.

After jogging up the old cement sidewalk, I knock once then twice before entering. For a brief second, the thought of walking into a widow's house of eighty years old bears down on me. I'm about to freak out a few seconds after I call out Kate's name.

"Kate."

Nothing.

When the freak out is almost to hit me full force, Kate's slender tanned legs round the corner, relaxing all of me.

"Pizza." She smiles gently at me, unhooking the towel from the top of her head, and points to the table, where there are plates and glasses set out.

My mouth goes dry. I go to speak, then am forced to tear my vision from Kate, who's walking closer to me.

"What kind did you get?" She's close enough I can smell the cherry and vanilla scent hugging her body.

I clear my throat. My mind is foggy and exhausted from the last few days. "Pineapple. All pineapple."

"Max, I told you." She flips the first lid of the box, and I swear she gushes.

Kate's hand goes over her chest, and without apology, she plucks a piece of pizza from the box. Pieces of sauerkraut dangle over the side as the tip of the slice disappears between her lips. She nudges the boxes toward me with a free hand.

I'm ripped from the fantasy, or should I say reality, of seeing her in shorty shorts and tank top with no bra, fresh from the shower. I grab a piece of pizza, not tasting a bit of it as she turns toward the fridge. Kate pulls three beers from it then goes back for a bottle of chilled wine. She pops the tops on the drinks and pours herself a glass of wine.

"How in the hell did you know the Sour Pig was my favorite pizza ever?" She grabs the glass of wine, taking a sip.

I shrug. "It's my favorite."

The box of pepperoni pizza goes untouched as we devour the other large pizza. Kate gives up after two and a half slices. I do my best, finishing off the rest while washing it down with Coors. The beer and pizza is a perfect ending to an exhausting few weeks. I do find myself wondering why Kate has beer in her fridge, but I keep it bottled down. I also notice the wine she's drinking is Moscato, but a different brand than I bought the night of the great fall that brought us together. The bottle looks way more expensive. I memorize the brand for future reference.

"I'm stuffed." Kate tucks her legs under the dining room chair. "I should've had a beer, but wine sounded so good."

I push the last piece of crust in my mouth. "You're a beer drinker?"

"Sure am. I don't discriminate, really."

"You're cute." I reach out my hand and rest it on her bare leg.

"You're handsome," she replies.

"And it's like we are in sixth grade again," I match her.

We erupt in laughter. When Kate gets up to clean our mess, I help her. After it's all put away, including the whole pepperoni pizza, Kate leads me into the living room. An oversized canary yellow couch fills most of the space. There's a tiny television and lots of artwork. Kate places her glass of wine on an end table, and I do the same with my fresh beer on the opposite end table. Kate plops down on the couch with a few decorative pillows plunging to the ground. I follow her as she does her best to tug me down. The woman would never have to pull. The fact is I'd follow her anywhere at this point.

I relax back into the fluffy cushions, letting the couch swallow me. Kate snuggles up to my side then reaches over for her glass of wine. Thoughts of tomorrow consume me one by one.

"Should I wear the suit or the button-up shirt I showed you earlier today?" I run my hands through her damp hair, loving the feel of her body up against mine.

"Truth?" She peers up at me.

I tip back my beer and manage a nod at the same time.

"Neither. You need to wear what you do every

day. You're not going there to impress the adults. You're going there to impress Finn. Just be you."

I nod.

And she continues. "Wear your favorite t-shirt, blue jeans, boots, oh—and comb your hair, of course."

I peer down at her to see Kate's caring eyes aimed at me.

"How did this even happen?"

She shakes her head slowly from side to side. "My daddy always told me what was meant to be is meant to be whether you liked it or not, so you better just enjoy the ride."

A smile turns up the corner of my lips. I couldn't agree more. "Thank you."

I brush my hand over the harshness of her cast. Kate let her students sign it. There are scribbles, initials, hearts, and various other symbols. I find myself rubbing the mathematical equation. I didn't have to ask to know it was Finn's. My fingertips outline each perfect line of his numbers and symbols.

"I'm so tired," I admit.

There've been, at best, only a few hours of sleep each night since coming home. Not to mention working my ass off day and night.

"I can imagine." She sets down her glass of wine and loops her arm around my neck, resting her cast over my shoulder. My hand goes back to the spot Finn signed on her cast. It's a symbol of pure innocence and perfection and comfort to me. Her other hand rakes through my hair. My first instinct was to get the shit cut off after years of being trained to keep it cut short and neat. It's not long by any means but still drives me nuts.

That's until Kate rakes her fingers through it, swirling her fingertips on my scalp, relaxing me with each movement. We don't say another word as we hold each other. I worry about tomorrow, and Kate soothes each stress away with her touch, warmth, and scent. I don't take another swig of my beer or move. The next thing I know, I'm slipping away into slumber.

Chapter 12

Kate

"Miss Kate."

I feel a tug on the end of my sweater and look down to see a miniature Max staring back at me. I squat down so I'm eye to eye with Finn. It's been torture not telling him everything will be okay.

"What's up, Finn?" I grab his hand.

"I forgot my special project in the room."

It takes me a second to figure out what he's talking about. We didn't do any art or sculpting projects today. Then it dawns on me he's talking about the book he's been writing. I haven't read a word of it because he hasn't offered to share it with me. A few months ago, he asked if I could staple papers together so he could write. Of course I did, but then he nibbled on his lower lip. Once I got it out of him, he was bothered because some of the pages were crooked, so during recess I bound a thick stack of lined pages, covering it with laminated cardstock.

Since then, he writes in it all the time.

I've seen some descriptive pictures and math problems. But he writes in it more than anything. I've been so curious to know what he puts in it but have never wanted to disrespect him. The journal has become one of his most prized possessions.

"Wait here, sweetie. I'll be right back." I squeeze his hand.

"Miss Kate, I only have three minutes before Harriet comes." Tears are welling up in his eyes. "We don't have time."

Harriet is the sweetest foster parent I've met to date. It's clear she cares for Finn in her gentle touch and extreme patience with him. She works closely with Finn's case worker, Frank. Those two are the brightness in his life right now.

"Finn, deep breaths, I'll be right back. You stay right here." I give his hand one last squeeze and make eye contact with the first-grade teacher. She gives me a nod, letting me know she heard our conversation.

I rush back to the classroom, avoiding eye contact with Gilly, who has still been doing his best to intimidate me. His antics would've worked if it weren't for Max's encouragement to stand up for myself. Finn's journal is right on top of his desk as if it was on his mind and he got distracted, leaving behind his best friend.

I burst back out the doors, knowing Finn will more than likely be on the verge of a meltdown, and I'm right. The tears are spilling down his round cheeks as Harriet walks up to him.

"Finn!" I holler over the mass of children scurrying to the buses or their parents and wave his journal in the air.

He wipes the tears rolling down his face with the back of his hand. Harriet rubs his back. I kneel once I'm in front of him.

"Here you." I turn him around and tuck it in his backpack.

"Miss Kate, it goes in the second pocket, not the first one," Finn stutters out.

"I know, honey."

Once the journal is safely in place, I turn him around and give him a hug. His life is about to change forever. The happiness inside me is overwhelming. It's so strong I can barely handle it.

"You're going to have a great day, Finn," I whisper in his ear.

His little arms squeeze tight around my neck. "I'm meeting a man today."

It's the first time he's mentioned it all day.

"I know, honey. It's going to be so amazing."

"I'm scared. I don't want to meet him, but I don't want to go home."

I soothe circles on his back. "Trust me, Finn. Please just trust me."

This has to be the hardest thing I've ever done to date. I have to fight back the urge to grab Finn's hand and go with him. This poor little boy needs stability, and he's so close to getting there. Max filled me in on all the DNA testing, interviews, and all the other hoops he's had to jump through. It's not over by any means, but things are looking up for him. I do my best to stay in the boundaries of friendship or whatever we are. I find myself having to bite my tongue to keep my opinions and advice at bay. It's more important to me to remain a piece of his support system than prying for all the detailed information.

"Okay, Miss Kate," he stutters.

"Time to go," Harriet announces.

I stand up, straightening my sweater, and grab Finn's hand. I walk with them over to Harriet's car. Finn crawls into the huge SUV in his tattered jeans and shoes that are way too small and worn.

A voice clears behind me, and I turn to see Gilly standing there with his arms crossed over his chest. I give him a nod and walk past him with chills racing up and down my spine.

I make it to my classroom, unable to focus on anything. I should be stuffing folders for tomorrow's literature centers but find myself staring off into space and watching the clock. Finn and Max should be meeting right about now. I have no doubt Max is nervous as hell and Finn skeptical about the whole situation, his little brain running a hundred miles per minute.

A knock throttles me from my thoughts. I look up to see Gilly walking into my classroom. I push my glasses up on the bridge of my nose and remain sitting in a tiny chair behind a U-shaped table.

"You have a minute?" he asks, sitting across from me.

No, you chauvinistic asshole, I think to myself. Lord, how I'd love to let the words flow from my tongue. Reality is he's my boss and I'm on the clock.

"Sure, what's up?" I muster out in my most carefree voice.

"Things are tense between us, and I just wanted to apologize for that. I never should've asked you out to dinner. It's made things awkward in our working relationship." He rests on an elbow on the top of his thigh.

I think he forgot about the fact he not only asked me out once, but several times and was relentless.

"Okay," I reply, having no idea what to say.

"And about writing you up, it was nothing personal. I have to be fair and enforce rules to everyone."

Pain pierces the tip of my tongue from biting down on it so hard. Again, he forgot to mention all the other times he reprimanded me for "snooping around," his words, into Finn's situation.

"I get it, Mr. Gilly. And I didn't take it personal. I'll continue to do the best job possible." I snap a folder shut, doing my best to keep my cool.

"Great." He stands up, unbuttoning the top button on his dress shirt. "I'm glad we had this talk, Kate, and always know I'm here for you."

"Okay." I nod and smile as politely as I can.

Nothing like leaving that dating door open. I ignore the reference and go back to my work. I don't look up to watch him stride out of the room. I only know he's gone once his overwhelming expensive cologne fades away. I slump, knowing damn well he's not about to make my life easy. Doesn't matter because I'm doing what I love and that's all that matters. And now with Max in my life, I'm not sure anything could get me down.

I give up on work and head home. I pace back and forth for hours, watching the time and my phone. Nothing from Max. He told me he'd text or stop by after the visit. I've tried soaking in a tub with my casted arm propped up on the edge, binge watching *Sons of Anarchy* on Netflix, and even went for a run.

It's now past nine, and my mind is running crazy. I've run my hands over my yoga pants a million times. I finally give up and grab a hoodie before thinking things out and take off for Max's house. There's no need to hop in my car since we live so close. The street light lit up the road as I jogged the few blocks.

Every light in the house is on while the porch is cloaked in darkness. The first step creaks as I step on it.

"What are you doing here?" Max demands.

I jump back, slamming my hands over my chest. "Jesus, you scared me."

"Go home, Kate," he growls.

I take a step closer and am able to make out the bottle of whiskey next to him. No cup or mixer in sight.

"Max," I whisper.

He doesn't respond with words. He picks up the bottle and downs a long gulp. He damn near misses the table as he slams the bottle back down. He's drunk. Piss wasted.

"What happened, Max?" I creep closer to him.

Even in his toxic state, I know he'd never hurt me. It's the opposite; he's the one hurting, in more pain than I could ever imagine.

He stands from the rocker, causing the back of it to crash into the side of the house. He sways back and forth until he steadies himself, then rakes his hands through his tousled hair.

"What do you want to hear, Kate?" he roars. "I

107

met my son today, a boy that has been through hell and is scared of his own shadow. He's in shit clothes. I've seen the pictures of his scars and all the fucking reports. I had to act like it was a happy fucking day meeting him when I felt all the guilt in the world on my shoulders. Is that what you want to hear? How big of a fucking failure I am? Well, there you go."

He throws his arms out to the side. I take a few steps and grab the bottle of whiskey. There's not much left in it at all. I pour the remnants over the railing until it's drained.

"Max, you're letting the reminder of your demons win. You're falling down that slippery slope toward repeating the cycle. You are better than this." I set the bottle down and step to him, wrapping my arms around his middle.

"It fucking hurts." He drops his head down to mine.

"I know. Trust me, I've watched him for months. I can't imagine what you're going through, but I do know this Max won't do." I squeeze tighter, hoping not to set him off. "He needs all of you. And that means you're going to have to digest that guilt and shame and give him the world."

We stand in silence for long moments before Max moves. He turns me around and guides me inside his house. The sound of a loud engine roaring fades off into the distance. I have no idea who it is and honestly don't give a shit. Max doesn't stop until we are in the middle of his bedroom. He lets go of me, steps back, and reaches behind his neck. In one swift movement, he has his shirt off and makes quick work of his jeans until he's left in only a pair of black boxers.

Then before I know it, he advances my direction, tugging off my hoodie. The smell of whiskey floats off him. It's saddening and intoxicating all at once. He stops at my sweatshirt and tugs me down into bed with him, covering both of us in blankets.

He pulls me to his chest, gently kissing my forehead. "Thank you, Kate. I'm going to need you."

I run my hand up and down his jawline. "I'm here. Anytime. I'll share a drink with you, have dinner, paint your damn house, but I refuse to watch you destroy yourself."

"He's so perfect. It's haunting, though, how much of myself I saw in him."

"Life is shitty like that, but just think, he's only in kindergarten and has so much of his life ahead of him."

Max places another kiss on my forehead while his hand roams up and down my back. And all I can think is, *Damn, I wish he would've stripped me bare.* Max might be the one needing me right now, but in an odd way, I need him just as much.

"He talked about you nearly the whole time."

That makes me smile. "Oh yeah?"

"Miss Kate this and Miss Kate that."

"I am pretty damn cool." I lean up and kiss his jawline.

"Damn, he's a smart kid. He knew right away I was his dad. I was shocked. He knew I played football. I guess Ally told him some about me."

"How did he react, knowing you're his dad?" I kiss him again.

"He didn't really."

109

Max's eyes flutter shut. There's just enough moonlight shining through to make out his facial features. I can imagine he's exhausted after the day's events and the whiskey he downed.

Soon his breathing evens out. I keep my palm on his jaw and whisper, "Don't ever do that again, Max."

Once I begin to nod off, I know I better get up and head home. I search around his room for a piece of paper, and when I don't find one, I'm about to head out to the kitchen.

"No," Max mumbles and thrashes in the blankets.

I turn to see he's still dead asleep as the thrashing grows more violent.

***

Max

Jesus, I slipped so close to the edge of never returning. Seeing Finn today was so overwhelming, and I couldn't handle it. I wanted to call Kate or go to her, but that just made me feel weaker and pathetic. Then she shows up. She saves me.

I see two of her the moment she steps on the porch. Her scent and touch sobers me right up, with more than just the whiskey making me sleepy with her in my arms. I breathe her in and ground myself, and before I know it, I'm out.

Visions of me young and dirty drift in, my mom burning me, the men in and out of the house. The scenes swirl into Finn's sweet face being battered and beaten. It's an endless cycle of my past, from being bullied in high school to my days serving the country. I wince and feel my heart shatter when I'm back there with bullets whizzing by and my brothers going down all around me. A searing pain in my calf, then me holding my best friend as he takes his final gasp of air. It's all too much making my skin crawl. I know it's a dream, but I can't pull myself from it.

"Max." Kate's delicate voice floats into the mass of never-ending nightmares. "Max."

Arms wrap around my middle, her hair flowing over my shoulders as she hovers around me. The horrible visions of my dreams have vanished, leaving only darkness behind.

"Max, wake up, baby. You're okay." Her hand cups my cheek.

I pull from sleep and shake my head. My heart pounds as I work to ground myself. I come face to face with Kate, hovering above me with concern dancing in her eyes.

"It was a nightmare. I'm here," she soothes.

"Jesus," I whisper.

This isn't the first time I've had one of these episodes. There've been several, just not any with Finn's face mixed in. It's the reason good sleep rarely comes and I find myself working during the night.

"Kate," I whisper.

This time, I don't warn her before I kiss her. I need her. Crave her to burn away the ache with her touch and scent. I lean up and catch her lips with mine. Kate falls into the kiss, taking charge like last time. I grab her hips, rolling her on top until she's straddling me, and kiss the hell out of her.

Kate rolls her hips, and I keep kissing her until we

are both left exhausted. And this time, my sleep isn't interrupted.

Chapter 13

Max

Ice cream cones and Kate was a very bad idea. At the time, it seemed perfect, but now watching her pink tongue dart out and lap the melting sweetness is about to kill me. I crunch down the remaining part of my cone and focus on the road ahead of me. It's an unusually warm evening, so we decided to go on a walk since neither of us are big television junkies.

It's been two weeks since I first met Finn. A lot has happened, yet it feels as though time is creeping by. I tossed all the booze from my house because I don't trust myself right now. I have no doubt I'm strong enough, but not right now and I refuse to become her. My mother. I'd never admit it to anyone else, but the counselor I'm required to see by the system has been helping peel away layers of shame and guilt.

"It's gonna drip." I lean down and lick the base of Kate's cone and finger.

"Thanks." She squeezes our intertwined hands. "Don't know what I'd do without you."

"Smartass." I can't help but lean over and kiss her cheek.

"Things still going good at school?" I ask.

Kate's reaffirmed things are fine, even though I can read her like a book every time she ducks the question. I have a lingering suspicion she's not being fully honest. I can't blame her for protecting what she loves. We are too deep into this thing for me not to march into the building and beat the shit out of her boss. And even I know that's not good for anyone, so I remain patient, waiting on her to share more with me.

"Yes." She swipes her tongue along the vanilla ice cream. "Gilly has been gone nearly two weeks at conferences and district meetings. Things are good."

"Who?" I ask. A door slams. We both glance over to the gas station on the main drag we are strolling down. I'd believed Kate when she told me things were good at school because we've been dining out in town, going to the hardware and grocery store together. This makes me proud that she's not letting her asshole principal have power over her.

"You dirty motherfucker," a high-pitched voice squeals.

The noise catches our attention. It's centered on a van parked in front of the only gas station in town. There's a blur of action.

"Get back here," a deep voice hollers out.

"It's him. The asshole who ruined my life."

The picture comes into perfect view. That's when I see a figure from the past coming my way. It's a

114

shell, a skeleton, but it's Ally. I recognize her eyes even though they're sunken in. She can only weigh about eighty pounds and looks like death warmed over, judging by the dark lines under eyes and the twitch in her lip.

I push Kate behind me in a protective mode. All happy and carefree thoughts of an ice cream walk down the main road are long gone. Ally's name has come up in all the interviews and hearings, but I'd yet to see her. She's barely a ghost of the person I remember.

"You son of a bitch. You think you can just come in here on your white horse and take my boy away. You pathetic motherfucker."

She's right up in my face, and I keep a hand on Kate's hip. She better not move.

"I can't believe you!" Ally tries to jab a finger in my chest, but I sidestep her, taking Kate with my movement. Ally will have to get through me.

I remain stock still. There are so many fucking words I want to spit at her but know it's a lost cause, just like my mother. I know if I let one word slip from my tongue, I'd choke this drugged-out bitch to death. She deserves no better. It's not me, and I know that. However, the feelings and rage coursing through me tell a different story.

"You don't have anything to say, hometown hero? I followed you to college, and you dumped me."

I remain silent.

Ally takes a step back. "Oh, I see you finally found your All-American Princess and now you are back to save the day. You'll never fucking get Finn."

All of my patience has run thin. I've kept quiet

115

about everything I can, and I'm not proud of the words that are about to flow from my mouth. But by God, they are the honest truth.

"You want money, Ally? Need to go get your next hit? I'll give it to you since that has been your only priority. I got you." I tug my wallet out with my free hand, freeing bills ranging from fifties to hundreds. Her eyes go wide. And that's when I know I have her. It's sick and twisted, and how someone has fallen down this rabbit hole so fast and far is beyond me. I was on the verge with a bottle of whiskey in my hand and I'll never do it again. I free all the bills and hand them her way. "Is this what you want to get your next fix? Take it all. Doesn't matter to me."

It's so sick and twisted, but I'm fed up with this game. I have two end goals in mind, and they are Finn and Kate. Ally and my past have no room in that picture-perfect family frame.

"Fuck you, Max!" Ally takes a slap at my face. I'm quick enough to dodge it. "I'm better than your once low-class status now hometown hero bullshit! Fuck you."

And with that, Ally stomps back across the road to the rickety, rusty van. Some guy helps her in, and they are gone. It grips my heart tight, knowing once upon time that's where Finn would have been.

I've learned his routine and the way he likes things. He's a bit obsessive. He's just so damn lovable, I go along with him. I'm pretty damn certain that boy has taught me more about algebra and theory than any college professor.

"Are you okay?" Kate's hand comes around to my front. Her nails dig into my soft t-shirt, the same style

I've worn since she suggested it.

"Your ice cream gone yet?" I ask.

"What?" I can sense the pitch of stress in her voice.

That was an ugly scene, one no one wants to ever experience. It took me back to the days when my stomach would grow tight and my fingers would tremble until the abuse was gone.

"I'll finish your ice cream for ya," I respond.

"Max."

I turn around before Kate has the chance to say another word.

"Give that to me." I snag the melting cone from her hand and take a big lick.

"This isn't funny." She holds both of her hands up, and they shake from her core. Her skin has morphed to a pale green. The fright dancing in her eyes scares me. "She's dangerous, Max, and Finn's mom. I've seen it time and time again where the court favors them no matter what they've done."

This is my fault. I've shared just enough with Kate, but not everything, knowing her dickhead boss has her job on the chopping block.

"Babe." I toss the cone into some shrubs and tug her to me, cradling her head to my chest and kissing the top of her head. "She will have no chance of ever having full custody of Finn after I'm done with her. At best, she'll be granted supervised visits and again—that's at best. I have no doubt she'll ruin her own chances."

Kate doesn't respond, simply lets me hold her. The question that has been haunting me comes back to play in my mind. *Why in the hell is Ally back here?*

Her family disowned her, so why would she move back so close to her hometown? I have no doubt there's an ulterior motive, and that fact is bugging the hell out of me.

Kate lifts her head. "She can ruin all of this for you."

"She can," I agree, running my thumb along her jawline. "But I refuse to let her. Nothing is going to get in my way, and that's a promise."

"And you don't break promises," she whispers.

"That's right." I kiss her forehead. "Now let's finish our walk."

Hand in hand, we stride down the sidewalk until the sun begins to settle beyond the horizon. I remind Kate that I'll be with Harriet, picking up Finn tomorrow. We have our second home visit where Harriet and an older gentleman, Frank, will be supervising, and if all goes well, the transition of Max moving in with me begins.

Chapter 14

Kate

"Miss Kate, do you think Max will like this shirt?" Finn peels off the jacket he insisted on wearing all day to reveal a football shirt.

I bend down so I'm eye to eye with him. "I think he'll love it, but do you like it?"

He shrugs his shoulders and averts his gaze. "Kinda. I got to go to the store and pick out a new one with Harriet. Max loves football, and we played catch the other night. It was pretty fun."

"Finn." I place a hand on his shoulder. "You know what he'll love more than that shirt?"

He perks up, hungry for the answer.

"You. He loves you and anything to do with you. You could wear a hot pink shirt covered in elephants and he'd be thrilled."

"Eewww." Finn covers his mouth, trapping in his giggles. It's such a rare sight that tears prick in my eyes. Happy tears this time for this little man.

119

"It's true." I wave a finger at him.

"Miss Kate," he says again when I stand to get the centers ready while the rest of the kids are at recess.

I now know Finn didn't want to go outside for fear of getting his new shirt dirty. That would drive him nuts.

"Yeah, Finn." I grab the stacks of baskets filled with cubes, ready to place them around the room.

"I saw pictures of you on Max's phone."

I freeze. "You did?"

I guarantee Finn quickly picks up on the panic on my face. He can read people like a book even if he doesn't always express it.

"Yep, he said you are his best friend." He scratches the side of his head. That action usually tends to send me into a frenzied panic, wondering if he has lice. "Why didn't you tell me?"

I sigh out loud. "It's complicated, Finn. I'm not sure what to say here."

"Adult talk?" He tilts his head.

I have no doubt "adult talk" in his world means something horrible, and I don't want him associating mine and Max's relationship with that category. I scramble for an explanation, knowing darn well Finn is smart enough to read through any lines I throw him, so I go out on the limb and give it to him straight.

I walk back over to him and take a seat next to him so we are on the same level. "Finn, I'm going to tell you the truth. I'm not sure I should be, but you're that important to me. Okay?"

He nods.

"I met Max because I went looking for him. I

wanted to find a safe home for you. And along the way, we have become best friends." I reach over and grab his tiny hand.

"Do you know he's my dad?" Finn stares up at me, and all I can see is a miniature Max sitting in front of me, not sure if he should be scared or excited for the future. Then another thought strikes me. This never happened for Max until he was in high school. It's a wrenching fact.

"I do." I squeeze his hand. "How do you feel about that?"

He shrugs and nibbles on his bottom lip. "I'm excited but know my mom will come after me again. And I don't want her to."

And just like that, this little boy devastates me once again. It's a real and honest concern for Finn. Hell, it's one that keeps me up at night. I have no doubt at one point in Ally's life she was a great person, but she let drugs and selfish need take over her true soul. I have no idea how to respond, so I settle for a hug and a corny joke, knowing what Finn's reaction will be.

"What do you call a shoe made out of a banana?" I stand up and go about getting ready for our math lesson.

"What?" He rolls his eyes.

"A slipper." I throw my hand up in the air with the punch line.

Finn rolls his eyes again and gets his math packet from my desk, since he's way above the class. "Miss Kate, a banana can't be a shoe. The peel would disintegrate and rot. It would be smelly and attract gnats. But you could turn it into mulch to use in your garden."

He shakes his head as he pulls out his pencil and opens his packet. I watch as his little tongue pokes out to the side as he reads the first question. Max learned that Finn had a neighbor for years who took care of him. It was perfect so Ally could go out and party her ass off. Francis was an older lady with no family. She read to Finn, fixed him meals, and even took him to the library. It was the perfect nurturing he needed to fill his soul.

The rest of my students come racing in from recess. I stand at the door, giving each of them a high five while reminding them to tell the recess duty teacher about all their little squabbles. The afternoon flies by, and before I know it, we are cleaning up and the class is lining up to go home.

I keep an eye on Finn as he goes to the back of the line like he always does. But today there's a pep in his step that only I notice. He lets a little grin escape then peers back down at his feet. He unzips his jacket and puffs out his chest a little bit.

I can't help the smile that plasters across my face. I know we are a few minutes early to head out, but I can't contain my own excitement. The line leaders and door holders get in place as I march the hyper students out to the buses. They know the routine, and that makes my heart happy. I have no idea how I'll let them move on to first grade at the end of the year.

Finn races up to me, grabbing my hand as I see each of the students off. The chatter and excitement of the end of the school day is always exhilarating. I feel a tug on my hand and look down to Finn.

"Do you think he's coming?" he asks.

"I sure do." I point to Max striding towards us.

My knees go weak at first sight. He's dressed in a thick hoodie, worn jeans, and messy hair that he keeps running his hands through. It's a nervous tic. But I'm pretty sure what strikes me the hardest are the pair of aviators resting on his face. Part of me is sad that his whiskey-colored eyes are hidden, but the other turns me into a hot mess. A crooked grin appears on his face when he spots us.

I notice Harriet is at the car, letting Max pick up Finn without her. Finn waves his hand in the air. I've never seen him so open and outgoing. Max jerks his chin and jogs across the crosswalk, earning a scowl from the crotchety librarian who should've retired ten years ago. He doesn't even notice it.

"Finn, my man." Max rushes up to us, holding out his fist.

It takes Finn a while, but he manages to bump knuckles, do a high five, and some other trick. "Are you ready for the big day?"

He nods, then strips off his jacket, puffing out his chest like a peacock in full stride. The smile that lights up his face brings tears to my eyes this time. I can't handle all of this.

"What's this?" Max drops to his knees.

"Got a new shirt. Do you like it?" Finn asks.

"Did they have one in my size?" Max asks.

"Maybe. We got it at Wal-Mart in Longview."

"Well, I'll be checking to see if they do." Max stands up, taking Finn's hand.

Another action that's a miracle. Finn allowing Max to hold his hand is a huge sign that he is already falling in love with his dad.

"Teach, how are you today?" Max grins wide.

Finn giggles, covering his mouth at the use of the nickname.

I shake my head. "Good, and you?"

"On top of the world."

"You two have fun tonight." I pat Max's chest without thinking and ruffle Finn's hair.

Max leans in and whispers, "Keep your phone handy. If all goes well, would you be up for ice cream with the two of us?"

I nod. Not sure it's the best idea. But at this point, I don't give a damn. Watching the two of them walk away stirs up all sorts of emotions in me. I want to run with them and watch the two of them interact so damn bad. I force myself to turn back toward the school building once Max has Finn buckled in the back seat of Harriet's car. Instead of hopping in the front, Max slides in the back next to Finn.

Before searching for Finn's father, I had been a month ahead in lesson plans with worksheets copied and ready to go. It was all I had in my life. Then when Max entered the scene, I went to being three weeks ahead to struggling to stay even two weeks prepped. As much as I hate it, I force myself to the copier room and bust out two weeks worth of lessons.

If you've ever had to stand by a copier and wait for it to finish the job, then you know how damn grueling it can be. I slip in an ear bud and press play on the Audible app on my phone, then tuck it back in my pocket. I'm dying to find out what happens to J.J. and Navy in *Whiskey & You*. I listen to it every night before falling asleep. I finally discovered the timer function so I don't have to scour to find my place.

The copy machine whines to life, spitting out papers. I use the *next job* function to scan several more pages. Before I know it, I'm paper clipping and stacking papers. I try hard to focus on Navy's storyline but find myself drifting off to thoughts of Max and Finn and how their afternoon is going. I can't wait until Finn gets to sleep in his own bed and relish and grow in the love of Max.

The sun has begun to set from the narrow window in the copy room. I have no idea how much time has passed. The piles of papers grow taller each minute.

I lift open the copier, placing a workbook in it. *Whiskey & You* has taken a turn for the worse, with the suspense being painful and gutting. Two large hands come down on each side of me. My heart leaps up into my throat as a scream rips from my body. I rip the ear bud from my ear.

A hard body presses into my backside then a growl echoes in my ear. "You just can't seem to follow rules, can you, Kate?"

Gilly. I relax a tick, knowing it's not some murderer loose on the town. I'm back on stage five alert when he presses harder into my backside, the copier biting harshly into my front.

"Gilly," I squeak out.

"I told you to stay away from him. He's trash. Nothing but trouble, but you don't listen."

I interrupt his seething. "Let me go."

My voice quakes, which in turn pisses me off. When I get angry, tears come, then I look weak, and it only pisses me off even more. It's a vicious cycle.

"Then you go and take your class out four minutes early, breaking another rule. You know when to take

125

them out, yet you feel you're above the rules all of a sudden. Is Max rubbing off on you?"

Even though my entire body trembles and shakes in fear, I find the strength to stand up for myself. "It's none of your business. Now let me go, Steven."

"I'll be writing you up, which equates to putting you on a plan. I suggest you start listening to what I have to say."

He doesn't move and is damn well making sure his station of power is well known. He's pissed that I turned him down for a date. This is all an entertaining game of intimidation to him. I, for one, won't be playing.

"I will not go out with you. This is jealousy, Steven, and you know that. You're finding stupid crap to write me up on because I won't date you." I square my chin, staring down the racks of construction paper in front of me, and prepare to enter war. "I'm with Max. You have no right to dictate who I date and don't. If you're so hurt by my rejection, then go for it and take this to the board. I'll be contacting the union lawyers, and you can damn well bet I have all of this documented."

His evil laugh ricochets from every wall and I'm sure floats down the hall too. It's now dark outside, and I know I'm the last teacher here, and Jan, the janitor, will have music blaring in her ears and could be on the other end of the building.

My pride has just centered me right in the middle of a war I won't be winning. Steven's hand moves from the top of the copier to roam up my side and near the side of my boob. It's enough to send me over the edge. I grab the lid of the copier and slam it down on his hand, whirling in time to escape him.

"Don't you ever come near me again, Steven. I'll be reporting you," I scream.

I forget all about the copies near the printer and take off, only to be yanked back by my shirt. The sound of the material ripping rattles me and stops me in my tracks. Steven's hot breath hits the skin on my neck. He grazes his lips along the same violated area.

"You go ahead and do that, and just see what happens. Everything you love will go bye-bye. It's the way things work in a small town when someone else has the power. It's your choice, Kate." Steven shoves me from the back.

I stumble over my two own feet and don't stop running down the hall until I hit my classroom. What in the hell just happened? I know he's a jealous man who is hell-bent on power, but this came out of the blue. There were signs, but nothing like this. I grab my purse, leaving my teacher bag behind. Grading papers is the last thing on my mind.

I don't even turn off the lights in my room before I'm busting out the front doors. I don't look back. My vision blurs the closer I get to my car. The tears are long gone, leaving only fear behind to taunt me. My tiny car comes into view, offering the first sign of relief. My trembling hands fight against me as I unlock the car and open the door.

"Miss Kate," a tiny voice sounds off.

I look to the side of my car to see Max holding a football and Finn waving, with no Harriet in sight. I freeze, fight like hell to control my breathing, and plaster a fake smile on my face, all the while glancing over my shoulder. I grab a sweater from my front seat, not having any idea how small or big the rip is in the back of my shirt, and tug it on.

Finn doesn't pick up on my panicked state. Max, on the other hand, does. I can tell by the way his shoulders tense and his knuckles grow white around the ball in his hand.

"We came to get you for ice cream." Finn beams with pride.

I clear my throat. "You did?"

"Yep, Dad—I mean," Finn blushes a bright red, "I mean Max made me eat grilled chicken and broccoli for dinner, promising we'd pick you up for ice cream since you're best friends and all."

"Broccoli?" I ask, crooking up an eyebrow.

"I had one." He holds up a finger. "Bite."

"Drenched in ketchup?" I ask.

He nods. "Come on, let's walk to the ice cream place," he begs.

I spot Max's truck in the lot and feel relief. There's no way in hell I'm walking right now. He must pick up on my cue and takes over for me.

"Let's take my truck, bud. We can get there faster," Max suggest.

"Okay!" Finn races for the truck.

If my nerves weren't shattered as hell, I wouldn't even recognize the little boy in front of me. He's happy, talking, and excited for life. He's a new kid.

Max walks up to me and leans in. "Are you okay?"

I gulp down a ball of nerves, remembering the encounter that scared the shit out of me. I interlock my trembling hands to keep them from shaking.

"I'll take that as a no. Are you able to go with us?"

he whispers in my ear.

"Yes," I manage to squeak out.

"Then once Harriet picks up Finn, I'll be expecting answers. No exceptions," he hisses.

"He's not staying?" That comment snaps me out of my trance as we walk to his truck.

"No, he can, but I want to make sure he's solid in it," Max replies and opens the driver's side door for me to slide into the middle.

Finn has already climbed into his booster seat and promptly buckled his belt. Max rounds to Finn's side, taking his time to make sure Finn is properly secured.

"Thanks, Dad—I mean Max." Finn drops his head, seeming to be embarrassed at his mishap.

"Finn." Max waits until he looks up at him. He has no idea that giving Finn his time is the most important thing he can do for him. When he looks up, Max continues. "You can call me whatever you want, Finn. Dad sounds amazing, but if it makes you feel weird, that's okay too. Okay?"

Finn nods and chews on his bottom lip. A sore is beginning to blossom. I mentally remind myself to remind him to grab his Chapstick I make sure is in his pocket.

"I like calling you Dad, but it's just weird, and I'm not sure if…" He trails off.

"I'll tell you every day that I love you calling me Dad. Finn, we have lots of time to make up for, and if you call me Dad, that will make it sweet, like the ice cream we are about to devour."

Finn nods and beams with pride. Max kisses the top of his head, making Finn's chubby cheeks blush. Max shuts the door and rounds the front of the truck.

I pat Finn's front pocket, and on cue, he pulls out the tube of Chapstick.

Chapter 15

Kate

"I'm ready Max-Dad." Finn licks the chocolate ice cream from his lips.

"Yeah?" Max zips up Finn's jacket then adjusts his backpack. "I'll talk to Harriet and the others, and we will set the date."

"Thanks, Max-Dad, for giving me time." Finn waves to both of us as he jogs over to Harriet.

Even after the day I've had, I can't help but smile at the name Finn came up with. Max follows Finn over to the car and hugs him before buckling him in. I relax on the exposed beam on the porch. I've always heard life can take a sharp turn and all you can do is hang on for the ride. Lord knows I've read about it in books, seen it happen on the big screen, and even heard stories from friends I went to college with. I never in my wildest dreams thought mine would veer off course, and even more so how wonderful it would be.

131

I close my eyes, relaxing for the first time today. I'm exhausted, and it just hits me like a damn typhoon. I could fall asleep leaning against this pole. His scent lets me know he's here, mere feet in front of me. I open my eyes to see Max nearing me. His hands go to my hips, and I wince. He lets go, then pulls me closer by my shoulders and kisses my forehead. Damn, those kisses are my undoing. I want more. I want all of him, especially after today. I need his warmth and his genuine, raw love.

He doesn't ask questions. Instead, Max unbuttons my pants, tugging them down just enough to expose the glowing bruises forming on my skin.

"Talk," he growls.

He's pissed. I'm not scared in the least, unlike earlier today with Steven. Max's anger comes from a place of friendship and possibly love.

"Max, it's nothing."

He places a finger over my lips. "It's not nothing. Now talk, or I'll rip up this fucking town until I find out what's happening."

I drop my head, center myself, and look back up to him. "You're right. It's something. Can we go inside?"

He answers by pulling me into his house. It's a place of perfection. Small, homey, and clean. Everything from the simple dining room table to the black and white family photos screams the heart of Max.

He leads us to his couch. We settle down with me wrapped up in his arms. I'm thankful he doesn't make me face him. I know deep down what happened today shouldn't be embarrassing. None of it was my fault. But I'm a strong, independent woman, and the events that took place earlier are humiliating to the foundation of my soul.

"It was my principal. He cornered me in the copy room." I decide between sugar coating the story or letting it all out. Max's strong arms around me coax me into spilling it all. "He trapped me between the copier and pressed his body into mine. I told him to let go of me, but I was ignored."

Max's grip around me tightens. He remains silent. The vibes he's putting off tell me he's entirely pissed off.

"He was livid that he saw me talking to you and told me he was going to write me up for taking my class out to the buses a few minutes early. I fought back. I really did, Max." Emotion clogs my throat. Pathetic tears stream down my face when I remember the sheer terror of the whole scenario. "I slammed down the lid of the copier on his hand, and I was able to escape, but he caught me, tearing the back of my shirt. He threatened me. Told me I'd lose everything if I filed a complaint. Told me he'd make damn sure of that because he holds power in this small town."

The silence is deafening. My body falls limp getting everything out. And the exhaustion before has tripled now.

"Did he hurt you?" Max asks.

"Yes, but nothing really bad."

"Did he put his hands on you?" he seethes.

I nod.

"What's his name?"

This question gets my attention. I turn in his arms and point a finger at him. "No way, Max. You are so close to getting Finn back. You can't go off your hinges in my honor and get thrown in jail. I know exactly what's going on in that mind of yours."

"What's his name?" Max grits out one more time.

"Do you promise?" I ask.

Max sits up, grabbing the sides of my face. "The only thing I promise is that fucker will never touch you again. And before you go on about me screwing up my chances with Finn, remember I served this country. I know how to fight, and I know for a fact there are other men who will defend a woman's honor in a damn heartbeat, whether they know them or not. It's called doing what's right."

I duck my head. "Steven Gilly."

Max explodes from the couch and paces back and forth, alternating between clenching his fists and running them through his hair.

"How old is he?" he asks, not stopping.

"I don-don't know," I stutter. "Around our age, I guess."

"That motherfucker." Max pulls back his fist as if he is going to attack the wall but thinks better of it. "I can't believe this shit."

"Max."

He doesn't stop.

"Max! You are scaring me," I scream, and it's the truth. He's unhinged like I've never seen in my life. It's like a burning inferno of pain from the past has been ignited inside him. The smoke of that torrid fire escapes from the actions of his pacing and jerking.

This gets his attention. He freezes and looks over at me. The anger fades right before sadness takes over. "This is all my fault."

He collapses on the edge of the couch opposite me, burying his face in his hands. His knee bobs up and down in a steady rhythm.

"Talk to me," I whisper. "This can't be your fault. Steven is a righteous asshole."

Max doesn't look at me, keeping his face buried in his palms. "I went to school with him. He was a bastard then, too. Made my life a living hell along with his buddies. Cole was the ring leader, but Steven was always there, throwing taunts and rocks and, as we got older, swinging locker doors in my face."

"Max," I gasp. I move without thinking. It doesn't dawn on me how he might react to my touch. I drape my arms around his back, linking my hands in front of him. "This isn't your fault. Steven was pissy when I started turning down his advances."

"Then he went full dickhead when he saw me with you. That's my fault, Kate, no matter which way you slice it."

"Okay, play it that way." I kiss the back of his neck, my knees sinking in the couch cushions. "You may have ignited his power trip, so what? He doesn't own me, and there's no way in hell he gets to choose who I love."

The last two words shock me, but they are the truth. I've fallen in love with Max. He's brought life back into mine with his determination and strength. He's taken care of me and let me into his life, and now it's a place I never want to leave.

"Say it again," he whispers.

I go out on a limb, saying what I think he wants to hear. "He doesn't get to choose who I love. And I love you, Max."

His knee quits jerking. Moments later, he raises his head and has me pressed back on the couch. He runs his nose up and down my jawline. Then he moves lower, roaming over my body until he's above my hips. This time, he strips off my pants along with my boots. Each piece of clothing flies to the floor. Delicate kisses cover the bruising then roam down each leg until he's kissing my feet and moving back up to my stomach. He peels my blouse up and over my head. The small tear on the backside rips more, highlighting our situation.

I ignore the noise and focus on us. Max does the same thing as he continues to kiss every square inch of my body. I run my hands through his thick, dark hair. It's my favorite part of him. It's always messy yet styled. He keeps threatening to clean it up, and I refuse to hear such nonsense.

His hands sneak around my back, then I feel his fingers fumbling with the clasp of my bra. We've kissed, slept together, and cuddled but have never gone further than that. This is a pivotal point. I don't want to waste one minute and sear each moment to memory forever. This is love.

He slides the straps down once the back is undone and frees my breasts. His lips seal to a nipple as he rolls the other one with his hand. He has my body searing with desire.

"Max, let me touch you," I beg, writhing underneath him.

He answers by grabbing both of my hands with one of his and pinning them above my head, being careful of the cast on my wrist. I don't even know how he makes the action possible. He takes turns between each greedy, pebbled-up nipple. I'm not shy about the way he makes me feel. I squirm and moan out each pleasure he bestows upon me. He doesn't relent until I'm on the verge of tumbling over a cliff of desire.

"Max, please," I beg again.

He releases my hands, and I don't waste a moment tugging his worn t-shirt over his head. The perfect round burn scars on his chest come into view. Without thinking, I lean in, placing a tender kiss on each one. This man is everything to me. I reach down, fumbling with the button on his jeans and managing to get his zipper down.

"Kate," he hisses in my ear, darting out his tongue and lapping it on the shell of my ear. "I don't have any condoms."

"I'm on the pill, and I trust you. Now shut up."

There's no way in hell a piece of rubber is going to come between us. I had no idea how much I needed him. Max lets out a loud groan as I grab his base and stroke him. I line him up.

"Please," I beg again, shamelessly.

"Kate, give me a second." He drops his head to mine. "I want you so damn bad that I need to slow down."

"No." I guide him toward me and push up.

He hisses and pushes in inch by inch until he fills me. Max keeps his forehead on mine while intertwining our hands and placing them above us. He doesn't move once he's inside me. One gentle kiss, then two before he speaks.

His gravelly voice pierces my heart with a scar I never want to heal. "I love you, too, Kate."

"Show me." I catch his bottom lip between my teeth.

And he does. It's slow and seductive, letting me feel each sensation. I wrap my legs around him, making him go deeper. He catches my writhing moans in his mouth as his tongue dances around mine. My nipples grow harder, pressing into his solid chest. I've never felt safer than I do now. My skin glows with pleasure, love, and everything right in the world…because of Max.

Something snaps between us. An invisible barrier bursts, causing Max to pick up speed. He slams into me over and over until I'm clenching around him and my nails are digging into his back. I'm blinded by the release that rakes over my being and shatters inside me.

"Max! Oh my God. Max!" I scream out shamelessly.

I feel him swell inside me, and moments later Max grunts and growls, picking up his pace. Another swell of emotion builds up in me, consuming my thoughts of joining Max.

"Kate," he growls out. "Jesus, Kate."

The same way the world brought us together, in one miraculous action, we fall together in a pool of genuine and rare love.

Max collapses on me. I absorb all of him, never wanting to move. He turns his head, kissing up and down my neck.

"Do you trust me, Kate?" His lips graze against the tender skin on my neck.

"Yes, without a shadow of a doubt, Max. I gave you my heart."

He leans on his elbows and peers down at me. "I vow to protect you. You have to trust me, okay? I won't jeopardize our future, but I will take care of this."

I nod, knowing damn well he will. I reach down and run my nails and one palm up and down his back while drumming my nails with my casted side up and down his sculpted sides, relishing the promised silence between us.

We spend the rest of the night doing things usually done before making love. We explore each other's bodies in every possible way. The last thing I remember is giving in to sleep, wrapped up in Max's arms.

Chapter 16

Max

I fucking insisted on dropping Kate off at work today, just to make a statement. She refused, and I didn't want to make her more upset than she already was.

After dropping her off at her car hours before school started, I go to the local coffee shop. While waiting on my order, I do a bit of research on Steven Gilly. Being the douche he is, he has everything on social media. Picture after picture of different beautiful women fill his feed. There are pictures of him and Cole with other douche fucks there, too.

I go back to her house, doing my best to keep my anger at bay. Kate is surprised I show back up with her favorite coffee. And damn, seeing her in a silk robe with her tan legs peeking out and damp blonde locks falling over her shoulder about undoes me. Took everything inside me not to march her ass right up the stairs and take her every which way I could.

After last night, I know for certain she's mine, and I'll never get enough of her. I left her house after a quick peck on her lips and, well, a longer kiss that I had to pry myself away from. I was shocked I was able to walk away.

Now I'm a few blocks from the school, watching the children bustle in. Steven is nowhere in sight, and that alone is a damn gift from God because I'm not sure I'd have the willpower to remain seated. Kate is easy to spot, with her wild blonde hair stacked on top of her head and those damn nerd glasses she makes adorable, not to mention her lime green cast.

Finn bounces up to her and remains at her side until she walks in. I'm unsettled as hell, knowing that creepy no-good asshole is in that building with my son and girlfriend. Shit, we never made it official, but I'm going with it, and to be honest, she's more than a girlfriend. I now know what my parents have. Never thought I'd find it after Ally put me through the wringer.

My phone rings right on time. Dad's name flashes across the screen.

"Hey," I answer.

"Where the hell are you?" Dad fires at me.

"At the school."

"Jesus, I told you to stay away," he growls into the phone.

"I'm just watching. I'll be there in a few."

I wait until every last body disappears into the large school building before pulling away. Dad and Cody are in the rockers on my porch when I pull in along with Brady. The three of them are best friends and have been since their high school years, no matter which direction life took them.

"Meet your new babysitter, baby boy Max." Cody stands and pounds his chest.

"Shut the hell up," Brady grumbles. "Will you ever grow up?"

The answer is no, and anyone who knows Cody knows this. He will always be the fun-loving playboy who runs the local bar. There are rumors that once upon a time he had his heart broken and never got over it.

"I told you to stay away from him." Dad stands and makes his way to me.

He's pissed off. There's no doubting that. He's been through hell in his own life and mine. Through it all, he's been by my side.

"We have a plan." He slaps me on the shoulder. "You're going to sit down and listen. This is going down my way, no questions asked. I'm not about to see you come this far only to ruin it with your damn temper and pride."

I nod, digesting his message. He knows me all too well. After living in a small town with an abusive mother and enduring the nastiness of the town, it's hard not to fall back on gut reactions. I walked away one too many times without reacting, and I'm done with that shit.

I lean on a pillar of the porch and listen to the men. They've brought a bottle of rum with them. I'm assuming that was courtesy of Cody. They pour ample amounts into their black coffee.

"Made yourselves at home, I see." I pointed to the open door then the familiar mugs.

"It's part of the damn contract." Cody swirls his

mug in the air. "You know, one of those random drop-ins to make sure you're not trashing the damn joint."

Brady rolls his eyes and opens his mouth, more than likely to tell him to shut the fuck up. Dad cuts off the chaos before it can begin.

"You stay away from Steven, and Cole for that fact. You don't speed. Hell, you don't even jay walk. You walk the line and focus on Finn and Kate."

I nod. "Sounds great and all, but you know how this game works, Dad."

I make sure to watch the tone in my voice, not wanting to push him any further than he already is. Might seem pig-headed the way he's acting, but since Jessie got Jules, his one and only true love, and their daughter, Whit, back in his life, he's been hell-bent on protecting them with all he has. Nothing touches his family, which includes all his kids, his parents, and Jules' Nana.

"Don't be an ass." He takes a long pull from his coffee, sputtering and struggling to swallow down the liquid. "Fucking Cody, how much rum did you pour into this?"

Cody only shrugs.

"Anyway," Dad clears his throat, "Brady's brother, Duke, happens to be the school resource officer. Doesn't care much for Steven or the pricks on the school board. He's let us know that Steven is away at a conference for the next five days. This gives us time. It also puts him in a big city where temptation will be everywhere. He'll dip his nose in that shit. Pictures won't lie, Max. We'll have him by the balls."

A dozen questions stream through my brain. I open my mouth to speak, but Dad cuts me off.

"Don't ask questions. The less you know, the better."

"Duke has his number, kid. There's no worry. It all works in our favor, as sick as this is. The chairman of the board and superintendent are at this conference with Steven in San Diego," Brady adds.

Cody finishes his mug of coffee, which is probably more rum than anything. "And don't fool yourself, Max. You were thrown back into this one-horse shit hole, but there are more of us wanting change than the evil. This is what we do. We fight back and stand up for what's right. Won't be easy, but good always wins."

"Okay." I grab Dad's mug, needing something to dull the rage inside me while I process the plan. He was right; I cringe at how much rum is in the black coffee. It takes just one swallow to let the rum do its job. "I'm in."

I pass the mug back and tell them about the night Kate had to pour out the bottle of whiskey. I go into detail about the bruising on her skin and finish off with endless stories about Finn. It's insane to think about how we've been in each other's lives for only a few short weeks, but I already have so many memories to share.

"Bring him over for dinner when you all get settled in." Dad stands up and pats my shoulder. "And keep Kate close."

Dad gives me a quick hug while I get shoulder bumps from the other two. Dad climbs into his truck, the same one he's driven since I can remember. It grounds me in an odd way.

He rolls down his window and rests his shoulder on the window. "And call your damn mom before she drives me insane."

"Will do." I give him a wave before he drives away with Cody and Brady.

I relax back into the rocker, staring at the coffee mugs and half-empty bottle of rum. Damn pigs making a mess. I damn well know Dad left that bottle behind as a message. He knows I have it in me to fight all my demons. That alone makes me believe in myself.

I clean up the mess, draining the coffee and washing the mugs, placing them on the drying rack. I place the bottle of rum up on the shelf above my refrigerator, feeling stronger, knowing I can do this with my support system. My demons have nothing on them.

I force myself to crack open my Mac. My business has been barely hanging on. I opened a division of IT support before my life changed forever. It's a money maker, including six employees serving large businesses as well as supporting their web pages. I pull out my reading glasses that I only wear when working on the computer. The damn things make me feel like a dinosaur.

The time flies as I jam to my old school playlist, knocking out my to-do list. Thank God I set my timer. I nearly jump out of my seat when it goes off. Today is the day. Finn's first sleepover. Harriet is going to hang with us for a while before leaving him. Between the shit show yesterday and this morning, I never told Kate. I'm hoping she'll join us for dinner tonight.

Which reminds me, I need to text Cody to make sure he can follow Kate home. That thought kills me, but there's no way Kate can sleep over tonight with Finn. Baby steps. They just may kill me.

I make it to the school just in time to see Kate appear with Finn scurrying up to her side. He glances around with a worried look on his face. I wonder if that will ever fade away.

I wave my hand, rushing up to him. Finn lights up and drops Kate's hand. It's something I never thought I'd see. His trust in me is natural. I thought I loved him at first sight. I had no idea.

"Max-Dad, you're here. You remembered." He races up to me.

Kate keeps an eye him the whole time while watching the rest of her students flee from the masses. She gives each of them a hug or high-five as they head home. I'm one lucky bastard, having these two unbelievable people in my life.

"Of course, I did, buddy." I grab him without thinking, wrapping him up in a hug.

His tiny body goes still. It was such a natural reaction. I kiss the side of his head before setting him down, then hold out my fist to him. We do our bro shake, then he grabs my hand.

"Oh no." Finn freezes.

"What's up, buddy?" I ask, concerned.

"I forgot Miss Kate." He tugs me toward her. "I didn't tell her 'bye,' and she didn't tell me to be brave."

"Can't have that happening."

Finn waits patiently as the other kids love on Kate.

146

His manners blow me away.

"Hey there, mister, thought you ditched me." She kneels, holding her arms out wide.

"Sorry." He drops his head.

"No, no." She squeezes him. "I'm happy you did, Finn. That's how it should be."

"Are you coming over tonight?" he asks.

I step in, answering the question for her. "She is. We have to get home and cook dinner for her."

Finn spins on me, pointing a finger at me. "No broccoli, right?"

I can't help the chuckle that escapes me. "No broccoli. Carrots and tomatoes, though."

He wrinkles his nose and shakes his head in disgust. As soon as Kate stands up with an amused smile plastered on her face, I lean in and whisper in her ear. I know there are several sets of eyes on us, so I do my best to keep it friendly.

"I want to kiss the hell out of you right now, Teach."

"Max, behave."

"Dinner at six?"

She nods.

"He's not here today. It's been a good day."

"I know." I lean back, making sure we don't linger too long.

She cranes her head in question.

"Trust me." I tuck my hands in my pockets to keep from pulling her to me. "And yes, he's alive."

I wink at her.

"Max-Dad, are we going yet? I see Harriet over there." He points and waves at her.

Foster care has a damn bad rap, and I have no

doubt Finn has experienced his fair share of negativity, but Harriet and the team she works with are phenomenal.

Chapter 17

Kate

I know Steven is miles away, but it doesn't stop me from looking over my shoulder every few seconds. I make quick work of tidying my classroom. I pack everything that I can complete at home in my bag. I don't want to stay here any longer than I have to.

It's a foreign feeling, not being the last teacher left in the building. I can count on one hand how many times this has happened. As I walk out to my car, an intense itch under my cast ensues. It's becoming worse as each day passes.

Planning on walking to Max's house for dinner, I indulge in a glass of wine in hopes of relaxing after the day at work. As usual, my thoughts drift to the two men in my life. Max was so relaxed today when he picked up Finn. Not going to lie, I was stressed all day about what would go down when he picked up Finn.

Knowing Steven is out of town at an educational conference soothes some of that worry. There's a lingering threat looming over me, and I can't shake it. The wine does help relax me and eases some of the worry and dread. Before I know it, it's time to head to Max's house.

Today is the big day where Max crossed all of his t's and dotted all of his i's in his battle to gain full custody of Finn. He came out the victor in the war; granted, Ally didn't put up much of a fight, but I'm sure she's not out of the picture forever. I refuse to let that thought have any power over the celebration tonight. Max went through the whole process with his parents at his side. I won't lie, it killed me a bit not to be involved as I would've liked, but in the end, it was for the best. Max had to do this for him and did one hell of a job.

I'm a guest tonight in Finn's brand new home. There's no way I'm about to go in empty handed. I purchased the largest bottle of ketchup I could find and tied it off with a bright blue bow. And you can't ever go wrong when bringing sweets. Finn may despise vegetables, but his sweet tooth is strong. I go for the homemade variety, straight from the local bakery. That's as homemade as it gets around here.

Max's quaint house is all lit up when I step onto the porch. I peer into the kitchen window that's cracked open, allowing the aroma of dinner to seep out, to see Max stirring a pot on the stove while Finn builds with blocks, sketching down ideas as he goes. If I didn't know better, I'd think they'd done this routine for years now.

I knock lightly on the door. I see Finn's head pop

up. He's off his chair and scrambling to the door.

"Hey." Max turns from the stove. "What did we talk about earlier?"

Finn drops his head. I'm hoping he bounces back from this like the other times he's dropped his head in front of Max. I know there's going to be a day where Finn has a meltdown. Everything right now is brand new and shiny. Max has been respectful to Finn's quirks. One day it will happen, and that will be the true test.

When Finn doesn't answer or make eye contact, Max continues. "You need to let me know when you answer the door. Once you have permission, it's all on you, little man. Okay?"

Finn nods.

"You're not in trouble. I just want to keep you safe."

"But it's Miss Kate," Finn replies, stepping away from Max.

"That's who we are expecting, but it could be someone else," Max continues in an even tone.

"Like a bad guy. One of Mom's friends?" Finn asks.

Oh, shit. Max's jaw ticks, and he visibly takes a few deep breaths before carrying on. "It could be anyone, and that's why I need to know."

"Okay." Finn nods. "Max-Dad, can I answer the door?"

Max glances out the window to see my face all but plastered to it, watching the scene fold out. I take his nod as a cue to knock again. The door whips open. Finn smiles brightly up at me.

"I was right, Max-Dad. You were wrong. It's just

151

Miss Kate." Finn waves at me.

I make a mental note to do a mini-lesson in class on answering the door and making sure their parents are always around.

Max shakes his head, continuing to tend the dinner on the stove top.

"Miss Kate, do you want to see our house? I can give you the tour."

"I'd love that, Finn."

"Oh, wait!" He dashes to the refrigerator, tugging down a piece of paper. "Look at my new name."

In his perfect handwriting, Finn James is printed front and center.

"I am so happy for you, Finn James," I say, trying out his new name for myself.

"Okay, but can you wait? I need to finish this." He bounces back up into the chair, darts out his tiny tongue, and goes back to his blocks.

This is a prime example of a Finn meltdown. If he were to be forced to leave his blocks and move onto another task, he wouldn't be able to handle it. I make another mental note to talk to Max about my idea of Finn being on the autism spectrum. Although I suspect he's on the high-functioning end, it will help Max better understand his son.

"Sure can. I'll see if your Max-Dad needs help over here." I make my way to Max as he's setting the cookies at his side.

He keeps his back to me as he stirs a red pasta sauce on the stove with large chunks of sausage and vegetables in it.

"Smells great, babe." I squeeze his side that's not visible from Finn's view.

"You do too." He looks over his shoulder and winks.

"Brought my famous cookies."

"They are my favorite." I can hear the mischievous tone in his voice.

I step to his side and lean on the counter, crossing my arms and facing him as he continues to focus on finishing the meal. "How's he doing?"

"Good. I'm no fool and know it's still the honeymoon phase between us. A bit nervous for tonight," he admits.

"You'll be fine. I'm clearly no parent, but I do know from teaching there's really no right or wrong way. You two will find this out as you go." I can't help myself and reach over, tucking my fingers in the waistband of his jeans.

Max in a tight black t-shirt, worn jeans, and barefoot, cooking dinner, is a sight that has me simmering just like the pasta sauce in the pan.

"Yeah, found that one out when I told Finn he could take his shoes off inside. He wasn't having any of it. The more I encouraged, the more frustrated he became. So I watched him toe them off, tie the laces perfectly once they were off, and place them right by the door. It took him several times to get them just right." Max shakes his head.

A timer goes off. He steps back, breaking our connection as he grabs a pair of oven mitts and pulls out perfect golden brown pieces of garlic toast. There's so much I could tell Max about Finn. It's hard not to keep my knowledge to myself, but in this setting, I'm the girlfriend. Girlfriend? Is that what I am? It feels like so much more, but that's the role I am in. It's not my place right here to explain what I think. Lord knows we have enough stress in our relationship already.

I bounce from my thoughts and help set the table. Max went all out with salad, garlic toast, steamed vegetables, and pasta with a tomato sauce.

"Okay, I'm done." Finn claps his hands together, staring down at his masterpiece. "Come see my room, Miss Kate."

"First," I grab the bottle of ketchup from my purse, "here's a congratulations gift."

Finn beams, snagging it from my hand and putting it in the cupboard. "Thanks, but we already have one."

Max clears his throat.

I shake my head at Max, not bothered one bit by Finn's reaction to the gift.

"Go show Kate your room, then wash up, okay, little man?" Max smiles.

Finn nods and walks down the hallway. I follow him, knowing it's his way of inviting me. I'd never tell him I've seen the room. Hell, I put it together from painting the walls.

"Look." Finn swings the door wide open. He races over to the bed and jumps up on it, staring down at the geometrical pattern on the bed. "I've never had one of these."

His last words are so hushed I barely make them out. "A room?"

I take a seat next to him on the bed.

He shakes his head. "No, my own bed. Mom didn't have one for me, and I had to share or borrow one when at other people's houses."

I glance up to see Max standing in the doorway, leaning on it, with his hands crossed over his chest.

I rub his back. "Well, look at you, then. This is very special."

He nods his head. "I really like it here."

"It's awesome. Can I tell you a secret?"

He twiddles his fingers together, still staring down at his lap. "Yep."

"It's my favorite place besides my classroom."

"Me too," he agrees.

I let Finn have some moments of silence to digest everything. I can't imagine what he's processing right now. His little mind must be going a mile a minute. This is a brand-new world for him. It can't be easy when his previous one was filled with nothing but trauma and abuse and was as unsteady as they come.

"I'm going to share some friendly advice with you, Finn." I stand up from the bed and kneel before him. "I know you very well. I know what you like and don't like. I know how you put ketchup on everything and that you need time to move from one thing to another. I also know you are very particular about the things you do. Do you know who doesn't know this?"

Finn replies with a simple, "No."

"Max-Dad and the soon-to-be new people in your world." I drop my own head, not sure how to move on or if this is even making any sense to him. "It's going to be hard learning how both you and Max-Dad react to things, but I want you to make me a promise that you'll do your best to tell Max-Dad these things. If you're feeling frustrated and want to shut down, maybe you can do what we do in the classroom?"

There's a reading corner in my classroom. Early in the school year, I realized quickly Finn needed it to get himself together. When he was overwhelmed or not ready to move on to a task, I told him he could go over there for a few minutes to collect himself. It helped in the transition when we were both still learning the ropes of the classroom.

He nods, and that's all I need. The floorboards outside the hallway creak. I glance back to see Max has disappeared. I worry my lips, afraid I've gone too far talking to Finn and giving him advice.

"Let's go eat. Dinner looks amazing." I pat the top of Finn's leg.

He follows me down the hallway. We round into the tiny kitchen where Max is sitting at the table with his elbows propped up on it and his chin resting on his clutched hands. He shows no sign of emotion. I can't read if he's pissed off or enjoying the evening, which makes me nervous as hell. I tend to read the man like an open book. Pretty sure the way he wears everything he's feeling on his sleeve is what first drew me to him.

"Looks amazing." I take a seat next to Max, leaving one open right across from me.

Finn's tower of blocks remains sitting at the end of the table. He closes his journal and sets it on the chair in front of his creation. A showdown is about to happen, and I wait with bated breath to see how it plays out.

Finn climbs up into the empty chair across from me. Max eyes the blocks, then Finn, and then back to the blocks. They clearly don't belong on the dinner table with delicious food surrounding us. Max asking Finn to put away the blocks would be completely acceptable and what any other parent would do.

"Ketchup!" Finn points at the bottle in the middle of the table, breaking the silence in the room. "Thanks, Max-Dad."

Max's demeanor finally cracks with a smile on his face. He gently scoops a small portion of each dish on Finn's plate, ignoring the hisses he receives. The loudest comes when steamed vegetables hit his plate.

"I want you to take a bite of everything, okay? You have to grow up healthy and strong, little man." Max adds an extra heaping of vegetables to his own plate and then makes a show of eating them first.

It's a great tactic but does no good. Finn props himself on his knees and reaches for the ketchup, proceeding to squirt generous amounts all over his food, leaving nothing untouched, not even the salad.

Max tenses. I reach under the table and grab his hand. Max says a quick prayer, even though he's already taken several bites of vegetables. It's symbolic of our relationship and the night we are having, reminding me of a favorite quote of mine from Annette Funicello. *"Life doesn't have to be perfect to be wonderful."*

"I have never had these kind of noodles. I love spaghetti noodles." Finn stirs the pasta around his plate.

"They're called rigatoni noodles," I say.

Finn shakes his head and rolls his eyes. To most, it may come across as rude and bratty. Not in his case, because of course he knew this and thinks everyone else should as well.

"I know, Miss Kate. They taste the same because the same ingredients are made to use them. They're just a different shape and thickness."

"And happen to be my favorite," I add, popping one in my mouth.

The rest of the dinner goes amazing as we enjoy the meal Max prepared, the only sound being our forks clattering against the plates. Finn cuts up each rigatoni noodle so they resemble spaghetti and devours them. He manages to get one itty-bitty bite of vegetables down—soaked in ketchup.

"Go do your thing, and I'll clean up since you cooked." I lean over and kiss Max on the cheek. "It was delicious."

We both look over to Finn to see if he noticed the action. He didn't. He has his head down on the table, staring at his blocks. His tiny finger runs along the bottom bright yellow one.

"Don't leave until I have him tucked in?" Max returns the kiss.

"Wouldn't think about it."

Max forces himself away from me. I hand dry the dishes and give it my best guess where they go. Max is as organized as they come. I'm not sure if it's from his time serving in the military, or if just maybe he has a bit of Finn in him as well.

Max has opened up about his time serving. He went through the gamut of emotions sharing stories. The pride that exudes from him about his service makes my heart swell.

I finish putting away all the dishes and wipe the counter and table. Max still hasn't appeared from the hallway. I notice the bottle of rum on the shelf and spot a half empty bottle of white wine in his fridge. It's the one from our first night together when I drank way too much.

My cast makes a loud clatter in the silent kitchen when I reach in for it. I'm walking, so why the hell not? I love indulging in a glass of wine after dinner.

There are no wine glasses to be found in his cupboards. I'm guessing I either drank straight from the bottle or used a plastic cup from his college. Hell, I could've drank from a wine glass and broke it; I don't remember the small details. What I do remember is all that matters. Max. His scent. Him holding me.

I sink onto his couch. The memories invade. This will forever be my favorite couch on Earth. If I have my way, Max will never sell it. I take a sip of my wine, enjoying the sweet and tangy chill of the alcohol. I could so easily fall asleep here without a second thought, but I know better. We have a deck of cards stacked up against us. I'm willing to be patient.

I'm one swallow away from finishing my wine when the hall light flips off and Max appears. He ducks into the kitchen and comes back with a bottle of water. The couch sinks next to me. He doesn't leave a sliver of an inch between us.

"You didn't have to clean it all up." He twists the top off the bottle and takes a chug.

I'm mesmerized at the way his throat bobs with each swallow. I could drink this man in all day every day and never get bored.

"Did he fall asleep okay?" I ask, snuggling into his side.

Max nods. "Yeah, he had to check the sheets and make sure they were tucked in. I'm fairly certain he was wanting to tear off the bedding and make a pile on the floor. It's what he's used to. I let him read me a book." Max chuckles. "I'm supposed to be the one reading to him. But he was damn giddy to read his book about sugar ants to me. Did you know those annoying bastards are mainly nocturnal and nests in holes in wood?"

I smile, loving hearing about his time with Finn. Even with the threat of bad times ahead, these precious moments have so much more power.

"I do know this, and only because of Mr. Finn, who explained in detail today while the other students were at recess."

"He doesn't go to recess?" Max drags his hand up and down my leg that's curled into him.

I take a second to relish in his touch. It has more power to make me drunk than the wine I consumed.

"Not really." I shrug.

"Why?" Max stiffens.

"Did you notice how he wouldn't leave his blocks tonight when he said he'd show me his room? And your story about how he had to take his shoes off? It's his tics. Typically, he's engrossed in a task and doesn't want to leave it. I feel, and I may be wrong," I pause, swallowing down the nerves that I'm about to broach this subject, "Finn's only safe place had been at school until now. I can't imagine what his poor body and mind went through when he never had a solid environment to thrive in. Finn is Finn. He processes things his way. I've never wanted to rip that away from him in the one place he feels safe."

Max clears his throat. "I don't know how to ask this, Kate. Anyway I do I'll sound like a dick. What's wr—"

I press a finger to his lips before he has the chance to finish his question. There's no easy way of asking, and I never want him to regret anything. It's not easy. I'm not even a parent, and I still know that all too well, from earning my master's in early education and the short time I have been teaching.

"Max," I twist to completely face him, "Finn is healthy. Finn is now happy. He is so smart it blows me away every day. Every kid has their own tics and the way they learn and thrive in life. There's nothing wrong with him, Max. The beautiful thing is he is unique, himself, and learns the way he wants."

Max drops his head to mine, exhaling harshly. I feel the stress rip away from his body.

"Thank you," Max whispers.

"You okay?" My lips brush against him with each syllable.

"Yeah." He kisses me quickly. "Want an ugly truth?"

"Always." I run my fingers along his jawline.

"I'd be drowning in whiskey without you. I need this and you." He pauses, kissing me hard. "A long time ago, I really thought I was in love. I was so very wrong. It stilted me and turned me into a man I didn't recognize. I found myself leaving on a journey that was calling my name. The part of my life that I thought broke me has brought me back to life. It's all because of you, Kate. You had the courage to call me. Reach out when nobody else would help Finn. You saved me. You saved us."

His lips crash into mine without abandonment. It's fierce and hot as we claw at each other, not keeping one single part of our souls at bay. We give it all. His taste invades my mouth with each sweep of his tongue.

Max flips us so once again he's on top of me. Tonight he doesn't strip me. He bares just enough so we can connect. It's all we need because we have everything right now. I wiggle my good arm down between us. I can't wait for this damn cast to come off. Only a few more weeks. I manage to free him.

Max doesn't ask for permission this time or take it slow. He thrusts into me like he owns me, and he does. His tempo is slow, deliberate, and precise with each movement. The tension inside me churns painfully slow to a slipping point.

Max swells inside me. It sends me over the edge. I want to scream and pull Max closer but settle for tugging on his hair as he spills into me. I'm nothing but a melted heap of limbs and lust.

"I love you," I whisper, continuing to drag my hand through his hair.

Max doesn't move. My eyelids grow heavy as his breathing evens out. It's the perfect lullaby.

Chapter 18

Max

"Where's Finn?" Kate asks, walking in with two boxes of her famous cookies she passes off as her own from the bakery.

I crook an eyebrow, close the distance between us, and have her in my arms before she can make a sound. Our sexy time has been limited. By limited, I mean zero to zilch. We haven't been with each other since last week after Finn went to bed. We had to be quiet. It wasn't hard, considering the moment we shared. I thought the first time was surreal. I was very wrong. In the back of my mind, Finn could walk out at any moment. The power of holding Kate underneath me had me on a mission no good man could turn down.

I've debated about taking her out on a lunch date, and by lunch date, I mean picking her up at school, bringing her back here to my house, and rattling the walls until Kate forgot her name.

"That's the greeting I get?" I drop my head, running my nose up and down the crook of her neck. She's beautiful from head to toe. This spot is my favorite part.

"Oh hey, M-Max," she stutters, dropping the boxes of cookies on the counter.

"Hey, you," I respond, roaming a hand up her baggy sweater until I'm cupping the swell of her breast in my hand.

Kate bucks into me, tugging my hair back. It's a sign for me to stop and continue on full force at the same time.

"Where's Finn?" she whispers.

I drop my other hand down between her legs, cupping her center through her leggings. Kate can't help but buck into my touch.

"That's it, baby." I move my hand, matching her rhythm, wanting more than anything to get this beauty off on my touch right now.

"Max, stop," she moans, writhing her hips harder and faster.

"That's it." I grind my hard-on into her thigh. "I want to taste you so fucking bad right now."

"I want you too, Max." My name comes out in a high pitch, then her body relaxes. The way she clenches my hand damn well lets me know she just had a damn good orgasm, courtesy of me in my kitchen.

"Can I have your cookies now?" I kiss her cheek, wink, and force myself to step back from her.

Perfect timing as Finn rushes around the corner with a bright red tie dangling from his pocket and his football t-shirt proudly on display. "I'm ready, Max-

Dad. Kate, you are here!"

I'm chopped liver as he races to her. He stops right before he reaches her; there are no hugs or high fives. He shoves out his chest in honor, then slicks a hand through his hair. Kate and I both bite back our laughter at the same time.

"How do I look?" he asks, tucking his hands in his pocket.

He has a hell of time with the right pocket as the tie gets in the way.

"Like a million dollars."

Finn rolls his eyes. "I don't look like a stack of bills. I look handsome."

"That you do." Kate smiles wide.

"Little man, did you want to wear that tie?" I sit in the kitchen chair next to him.

He rolls his head back and forth. "I like it, but it looks good hanging out of my pocket."

I concentrate on inhaling and exhaling. A tie is made to be worn around your neck while in a dress shirt. It looks ridiculous hanging out of his pocket. I fight back the urge to pursue a conversation about this. Finn wins every time, and I'm okay with that, because like Kate said, he's happy and healthy.

"Don't you think, Dad?" Finn tilts his head, waiting anxiously on my answer.

Now I'm having a hard time breathing. It's the first time he's used the term of endearment without stuttering over it or creating a new nickname. We've had a whole week in the house together. It's been perfect, tough as hell, and so very worth it all at the same time.

I've watched him drench his macaroni and cheese

in ketchup, hide his new backpack in the closet so nobody would steal it, and second-guess climbing into a bed every night. All of it tugged at my patience. I wanted more than anything for my son to be like other kids his age who are worried about the latest trends, begging to go on play dates, and enjoying the mud while they splashed around in it. I was so very wrong in my thoughts about what an ideal son looks like. Finn keeps proving this fact over and over again.

"I couldn't agree more." The four words barely come out through my emotionally choked throat. "It's perfect."

And that's the honest to God truth. I've never been surer about anything else before.

"Hey, don't we have to be in Boone in like ten minutes?" Kate asks.

"We do!" Finn jolts for the door. "I'm going to meet people. I have people to meet. Let's go."

I grab Kate's hand and we follow Finn to my truck. I voice out loud my internal concern. "Let's hope he's this excited when we get there."

Kate, ever my voice of reason and love, assures me he won't be.

"Yeah, won't happen. It will take Finn time to warm up. He loves the idea of meeting new people in a safe place, but he will become overwhelmed."

"Maybe not." I wink at her. "My family has a damn good way of prying any wayward person right out of their comfort zone."

I get Finn all settled in his booster seat. Freaked the shit out of me when I read about kids under a certain weight and age should never ride in the front seat. After researching, I realized it was because of the airbags. Well, this old piece of metal doesn't have any of that shit.

Kate slides into the middle, and Johnny Cash entertains us on the drive. Not a word needs to be spoken.

"Dad!" Finn screams.

On instinct, I slam on the brakes. A horn blares bchind me as I jerk the truck off the road. I glance over to Finn with a thousand horses stampeding over my heart. His tiny finger is pressed against the window.

"That's the same store where Harriet bought me my football shirt. Not the same exact store but the same one," he proudly announces.

I grip the steering wheel until my knuckles grow white. Kate's hand remains over her chest where she slapped it when she thought we were dying. My nostrils flare, relieving some of the panic and anxiety that just went down.

"Do you want one like mine?" Finn asks, keeping his finger pressed to the window while craning his neck to look at me.

"Yeah." I clear my throat. "I sure do."

I pull the truck into the parking lot. Finn is all business, leading us to the section of t-shirts just like his. He told us the store is laid out opposite of the one he was in. He went on about if you flipped you'd go right instead of left. Me—I'm still rattled from being scared to shit when I heard him scream.

It caught me off guard. Now, looking back, I know it was one of excitement and not panic.

We find an XXL in the youth section, and I'm

bound and determined to fit into the bastard if it's the last thing I do. Kate takes Finn out to the truck when I go into the bathroom to change out of my favorite college t-shirt that's worn and well-loved into a stiff and scratchy generic football one. I couldn't be prouder when I get the thing stretched out over my shoulders. I could give a fuck less if it's tight there, but I refuse to wear a belly shirt even for Finn.

Thankfully, it's long enough. On the downside, I look like a dude who's been working out and over eager to show off his new muscles. I shake my head at my reflection in the mirror. This right here is true damn love.

I strut out into the parking lot like a peacock with shiny feathers. I spot the van first, then see a flash of blonde hair as Kate races to the truck. I run faster than I ever have. Adrenaline courses through my veins. If one hair is hurt on either of them, Ally will see what the true Max is capable of, and I won't even blink when I do finish her.

I fling open the driver's side door, on guard and ready to take care of business. I step back when I hear Finn's laughter echoing around the cab. Kate pats the seat next to her, which is the driver's seat. I'm still too stunned to speak yet keep an eye out around us.

"I told you, Miss Kate. I'm a faster runner than you. It doesn't matter if my legs are shorter."

I study Finn's unharmed face and body. It's his smile and carefree giggle that follows that eases all of the concern cemented on my shoulders.

"You were right. I just knew I could beat you," she replies.

I climb into the truck, confused as hell. Kate grabs

my free hand, giving it a reassuring squeeze as she pats the top of Finn's kneecap with her casted hand.

"Let's go. Nothing else for us here." She beams proudly.

There's a story, and I can only guess that she spotted the van and possibly Ally. Then my quick-thinking woman challenged Finn to a race.

"I even beat you holding your hand." Finn slaps his other knee, clearly amused with himself and oblivious to everything around him.

My suspicions are confirmed once we pull into my parents' driveway and Kate slides out after me. She perches up on her tiptoes and whispers in my ear.

"It was the same van. I heard Ally but never saw her. She was screaming. That creepy guy was with her. Finn was rattling on about facts where he had to stop and count them off on one hand. Then he went on about you two in matching shirts. The van came closer into view, and I knew beyond a doubt it was them. He never heard her. That's when I decided to declare a race."

"Thank you." I reach back and pat her ass before going to help Finn out of the truck.

Well, there's no helping Finn; he has a systematic method to everything, including getting out of the truck. I wait for him, relishing the moments I get to watch my son be himself. I wouldn't want him any other way.

A sweet little voice streams from the porch. "We ain't buying any."

I glance up to see Emma in a tutu with her sass on full force. Talk about a kid marching to her own drum. Emma doesn't care what others think. She

169

does what she wants and asks for no apologies. I love my little sister. My parents have never tried to change or mold any of us into their own vision of perfection.

"Oh, it's Max." She dramatically smacks herself in the forehead. "My Bubba."

She races down the steps, bounding along the sidewalk until she's at my side. Finn stares her down with fierce abandonment. Gasoline meet fire. Shit is about to get real.

Emma sticks out her hand. "I'm Emma Jane, and who are you?"

Finn takes a step back and points at her hand. "I'm Finn."

Emma pretends to shake his hand. "It's nice to meet you. Want to see my swing?"

I'd give anything to stick a plug in her mouth. There's no stopping her. She's a tidal wave that crashes without warning. Finn hasn't even had the chance to get his sea legs steady underneath him.

The smacking of the screen door alerts me to the fact others have joined us. I glance up to the porch to see Mom and Dad smiling wide. Kate rounds my side.

"Who is she?" Emma points. "Oh, duh, I know Kate."

Emma rolls her eyes and slaps the fluff of her tutu. Oh, the theatrics. Mom and Dad better get ready to roll into Hollywood with this one. There's no stopping her. She's a miniature Whit with sass multiplied by one thousand.

"Hi, Emma." Kate waves. "I love your tutu, and I'd love to see your swing."

There's my girl, saving the day with her gentle

care. It's natural. It's her. And that's why I love her. Emma forgets all about a little boy near her age and bounds off with Kate. Her chatter echoes around the farm.

"Was that your sister you told me about?" Finn asks, climbing back up into the truck.

"Sure is, little man, and I don't blame you for taking shelter."

He settles back into his booster seat. "She's loud."

"That she is," I reply.

"And kind of annoying." Finn picks at the laces of the shoes he refuses to get rid of.

"More than annoying," I add. "Want to know why?"

This gets him to quit picking at the laces, but he doesn't look at me. I carry on.

"She's used to old, boring people around this place and got just a bit too excited when she saw you."

Finn doesn't move or say a word.

"You know I'm an old guy. You told me the other day how many years I have left until I get the senior discount at McDonald's, and that's what she's used to around here. Can't blame her for being all jacked up, seeing another cool kid around her age."

"She's older, Dad. You know it. Older kids are mean."

"Yeah, they can be. Won't deny that, but one of my best friends was two years older than me."

"The one from the military that always tried tripping you when you walked out of the bathroom?" Finn glances up at me.

This kid is a sponge. I find myself telling him

every story I can, and he doesn't forget a bit of them. For now they're happy and funny stories he can relate to, but as he gets older, I'll share the stories that aren't so easy on the heart. The ones that made me who I am today.

"Yep, that one." I hold out my hand. "Want to meet my mom and dad?"

"Will you keep Emma away from me?"

I chuckle. "I'll try, but I'm only human."

I help Finn ease out of the truck. He taps the sides of it and pats his booster before walking away. His tiny hand squeezes mine so tight that I can feel his nerves mingle with my own.

"Did I mention my mom doesn't make any little kid eat vegetables?" I look up to see Mom and Dad with huge smiles on their faces.

I can tell they're antsy as hell to rush to Finn but hold themselves back.

"She doesn't?" Finn stops and looks up at me.

I know this is a big deal in his book, and he's studying me to see what my next play is. He's been around the block and is no fool.

"She'll cook them, don't get me wrong." I lean down as if I'm whispering a huge secret. "But she's not a pusher of them. The whole bowl will go uneaten tonight."

"Hey." Dad opens the gate.

I squeeze Finn's hand and go for it. "Dad. Looking old as hell!"

"You wish." Jessie wraps me in a tight hug.

"He's scared." I give him my best one-armed hug.

"We got this." He pats my back three times then steps back. "And who is this?"

Finn keeps his stare focused towards his battered sneakers. Mom clears her throat.

"Look at that, honey. Finn has a football on his shirt just like you."

This gets his attention. Finn lights up seeing the common tie.

"I'm Jessie, little man." Dad extends his hand while kneeling to Finn's level.

Finn extends his hand. No pretend handshake here. "I hate football. It looks like it hurts. I'm wearing this because my dad likes football and I wanted him to like me."

I seize in pain.

"Well, I've been told," Dad stops, stroking his beard with his fingers, "that only weirdos play with a football anyway."

Finn covers his mouth, trying to hide his giggle. It doesn't work; the sweet sound echoes around.

"And look at your dad, he has the same shirt on. So we must be doing something right."

Finn has warmed to Jessie, which is no shock at all. Now Mom steps up, speaking slowly. I know it's to keep her from sweeping Finn up in her arms.

"Tonight we are having candy, ketchup, and popcorn for dinner." She extends her hand.

Dad groans, knowing damn well he just got outplayed by his wife. That's Mom for you, and she never takes back her word.

Finn clasps her hand and shakes it. "Finn, these are my parents, Jessie and Jules."

One day I'll share with him the story of how they saved me and what I went through. I'll save my story until the day I need to use it as a gift to help empower

173

Finn. There will be no pity or sorrow involved.

"Come on in." Mom waves us in, and Dad wraps an arm low around her waist as we follow them.

Emma has Kate in the swing while telling her a wild story about something. Finn tugs on my hand and points over to them.

"Want to join them?" I go out on a ledge.

"Yes."

"Go for it. I'll be on the porch."

Finn drops my hand. He doesn't run like most children his age would. Instead, he's precise about the way he takes tentative steps over to the fun. Finn doesn't join in right away but stands back, watching the action with caution.

Emma's voice drifts by everyone once in a while when the breeze carries it. When the topic of aliens comes up, it piques Finn's interest. He steps right in, and I can only imagine him adding either common sense to the conversation or going on about a wild conspiracy theory. The longer the two sink deeper into conversation, the more I see Kate back away from them.

"They gonna make it or fight each other?" I ask when Kate takes the last steps with finesse and grace.

"I think they're going to become inseparable once they both realize their love for random facts." She goes to sit in the rocker to my left. I catch her hand before she does, tugging her into my lap. Kate doesn't protest; instead, she curls up into me. I gently rock back and forth as we listen to Emma and Finn play.

I palm Kate's ass and groan. It's torture having her so close. All I want to do is ravage the hell out of

174

her. "I'm thinking once Finn discovers Lego hell in Emma's room after dinner that you and I will be able to sneak up to my room."

"You want me to play with your Legos?" Kate pats my chest and giggles.

"Oh, babe, I want you to touch them, lick them, and do anything you want with them."

"Max." She slaps my chest. "We are not going to fool around in your childhood room while your parents are in the house. That's just wrong."

"I didn't say a damn thing about fooling around. I'm going to take you anyway I want."

***

Kate

This house is one from any heart-warming television show. It's so different from the one I grew up in as an only child. It's clean, but there's also a sense of organized chaos. Cheerleading gear can be found in every corner along with football pads, toys, random clothes, and an abundance of love and chaos.

Everyone's guards are down. I'm no longer under the microscope, being analyzed whether I'm going to ruin Max and rip his heart from his chest. The attention is focused right where it should be: on Finn. Jules came through with candy, ketchup, and popcorn for dinner. I didn't miss the proud as hell smile on Max's face when Finn asked for a slice of meatloaf and a half scoop of salad. Of course, he nibbled on a piece of lettuce. Okay, he actually licked ketchup off of it.

Emma begged her parents to go buy her a shirt like her brother's and Finn's until Jessie gave in. I had no clue what had happened until a young football player showed up at the door with a grocery sack in his hand and big smile on his face.

"Coach, here you go." He extended the bag out.

"No laps Monday, don't do anything stupid, and stay safe," Jessie responded.

Jules snapped several pictures of Emma and Finn in their t-shirts.

"I don't like football," Finn announces when she snaps the final one. "It's pretty boring to me."

Emma squeals in delight. "We are BFF's for life. I hate football. It is boring. The games take forrrrever. It's usually cold. Jack and Whit ditch me for their friends. It's so borrrring."

Jessie groans and tips back his drink. Jules shakes her head with a broad smile on her face.

"Want to play in my room?" Emma asks, running her hands down her new football shirt.

Finn looks over to Max, not saying a word. Max is up on his feet, walking over to him. Emma guides the two down the hallway. Max is only gone for five minutes before he returns.

"I'd say those two are getting along just fine," Jules announces.

"Yeah, they are." Max sinks down on the couch next to me, nearly pulling me into his lap. "Emma saved the day by assigning Finn a bin of Legos while she'll build out of another."

"He's a great kid, son," Jessie adds.

"He's perfect and so sweet. It took everything in me not to hug the hell out of him," Jules says. "Oh,

176

what happened with your principal?"

Jules looks at me, waiting on an answer. I open my mouth and snap it shut, having no idea if Max told them about Steven. In my gut, I know he didn't. But what in the hell is she talking about? Jules continues when I don't respond.

"I was down at the courthouse getting license plates for Whit's car. Don't tell her. It's a surprise. I overheard that the principal, superintendent, and board chairman over at your school have been indicted with charges. I was shocked."

I peer up at Max, studying his face, wondering if he had any idea. Steven has been quiet. Hell, non-existent since he pressed me into the copier and tried intimidating me into bending to his will.

I fumble with my fingers. "Honestly, I have no clue what you're talking about, Jules."

"I do," Jessie pipes up. "It was the talk at coffee this morning. I guess the three of them found themselves in a bit of trouble while away at a conference. There are pictures and everything. The assistant superintendent here in Boone said it sounded like their certificates would be revoked and jail time would be served. Don't know all the details, though."

Jessie is cut off when his cellphone begins to blare. He answers it, nodding his head and rolling his eyes. "I'll be there in a few, Whit."

Whit and Jack took off right after dinner. They love Max, there's no denying that fact, however, they're at an age where their social life is the most important thing.

"Everything, okay?" Jules asks.

177

Jessie stands up. "Yeah, Whit forgot some shit for the competition tomorrow. I'm going to run it over to her."

"I knew it was a bad idea having her stay over at Lisa's the night before a competition. They're going to stay up way too late and probably forget half of their stuff at her house in the morning."

Jessie kisses the top of Jules' head, squeezing her shoulder. It makes me smile, knowing exactly where Max gets that tendency.

"I'll be right back. Don't leave until then." Jessie picks up a large duffel bag embroidered with Whit's name by the door. It looks like she forgot her entire closet, not just one item.

"I'm going to hang with the cool kids." Jules pops up. "No offense."

"None taken, Mom."

Once Jules disappears, Max is up and on his feet, tugging me behind him.

"Max," I hiss, trying to pull back, but he doesn't stop.

We are up the stairs and entering the room in the far corner, furthest down the hall. Once the door shuts, Max grabs me by the hips and tosses me on the bed. I can't help the giggle that escapes me. The click of the lock on the door echoes around the room.

"Max, I told you we can't do this here."

"And I told you we are going to do this here." He tugs off each one of my boots, pulls down my jeans, and tosses them to the side, then my sweater is gone. Panties and bra are next until I'm bare before him.

This should be awkward since we are in his parents' home. It's not at all. The moon shines in the

178

room. I'm wrapped up in his scent and able to make out Max as he strips his own clothes until he's completely naked before me.

My breath hitches in my throat when he reaches down and strokes himself from base to tip. "We don't have all night, but just enough time, baby. I want you to ride me. Haven't been able to think of anything else for a damn long time."

Max advances on me, covering my body with his. Our lips connect and hands roam up and down each other's bodies. He flips us over so I'm on top of him. This is new and freaking brilliant. I press my palms into his chest and lean up for a second.

"Did you know about Steven?"

He shakes his head. "Knew something was going to go down but had no idea it had."

"So that was you?"

"Told you, babe, that he'd never hurt you again."

I slide down Max's body, raking my nails along, being careful not let my cast slide down along him. I grab him in my hand and thank him the best possible way I know how.

"Kate, damn." His hands twine in my hair, guiding the motion.

I swirl, lick, and ease the pressure then suck harder with each of his hushed moans. It fuels me on.

"Ride me, baby." Max pulls me back up to his face. He's devouring my lips before I have the chance to protest. The next thing I know, he slides into me. My head spins as he moves in and out of me.

Our lips separate, and Max runs a hand up my face, cupping my cheek. "Now ride me, Kate."

I plant both hands on his chest, not caring if the

cast is a burden or hurting him. I'm selfish in this moment, with the pleasure all too consuming. I'm in control, free, and have the man I love underneath me, hypnotized by the roll of my hips. It doesn't take long before I'm forced to bite down on my bottom lip to catch the scream of pleasure ripping through my body. It rattles everything from my head to my toes.

I feel nothing but sheer bliss until Max's fingers dig into my sides. His growl is low and guttural. He doesn't hold back but pumps everything inside me. It's nothing but perfection.

I collapse on his chest, relishing in the way he drags his fingers through my hair. I'm exhausted and fueled like always after Max and I connect. But a huge burden has been lifted from my chest. I'll no longer have to glance over my shoulder at school or worry about the hammer coming down on my job at any point, ripping me away from one of the things I love most. I'm free.

"Quit worrying," Max mumbles. "I can practically hear your thoughts."

"I'm not." I tilt my face up to him. "I'm relieved."

"You still need to go in front of the school board with your union lawyer and tell your story. It needs to be documented, and most of all, you need to be freed of the burden."

I nod, not excited over the fact I'll have to face the board, but he's right.

"And as much as I hate to break up this miniature version of a sleepover, we'd better get back downstairs," he adds.

I growl but agree once again. Max, being the gentleman, sits up with me in his arms and carries me to the bathroom connected to his room, letting me wash up first.

"Don't worry, no one will walk in. We all have our own bathroom."

Just the thought he planted in my head has me racing to clean up and get dressed. I've never been busted by a guy's parents, and having that happen now would be mortifying.

We walk back downstairs hand in hand. The Lego party has moved out to the living room. Finn is entranced, building an intricate tower while Emma creates simple stacks, entrapping all of her stuffed animals. Jules sits on the couch with a glass of wine watching the two of them and giving us a curious stare.

"Where did you two run off to?" She quirks up a brow.

"Gave her a tour," Max replies coolly, while I'm dying on the inside. We've been busted, and it couldn't be anymore obvious.

"Poured you a glass." Jules points to an end table. "Wasn't sure if you enjoyed wine or not."

"Thank you." I brush my hands down the front of my pants to keep my hands from roaming over my freshly screwed hair. "I do."

"Dad." Finn whirls around from his concentrated stare.

Jules smiles wide at the term of endearment, and Max is at Finn's side.

"What's up, little man?"

Finn's breathing picks up, his brows scrunch, and I know he's on the verge of a meltdown. "I, I need my—"

181

He has a hard time getting the words out through the frustration building up on the inside of him.

"Tacos," Max says. "Tacos."

Finn squeezes his eyes shut and centers himself.

"Tacos?" Emma queries, with puzzlement plastered on her face.

"Come here, honey." Jules pats her lap.

Emma isn't all too happy about it but minds her mother. She climbs up in her lap, giving Max and Finn space. I take a spot on the overstuffed chair, soothing my hand on the ottoman in front of it.

"Once you can get it out, tell me," Max encourages Finn.

He squeezes his eyes shut. "I need my journal, Dad. I can't build without it. I need to document this."

"Your journal?" Max asks.

He nods his head.

"Would a piece of paper or a fresh notebook work?"

He shakes his head.

"Don't want to give it a try?"

"No! I need my journal."

"Tacos," Max whispers.

Finn struggles to center himself.

"I'm proud of you, Finn. You're doing great. Your journal is in the truck in your backpack. I'll run and get it."

Finn doesn't react. Instead, he sits, focusing on his breathing as Max gets up from his side. I relax back in the chair, grab my wine, and kick my feet up on the ottoman, realizing we left my boots up in Max's room. A slight blush creeps on my face while pride overtakes it. How Max just worked Finn through a crisis was beautiful. He pushed him just a bit, and it seems the two of them came up with a coping strategy.

"You're in seventh grade, right, Emma?" I take a sip of the wine and damn, it is good. The kind of delicious where it would be easy to drink a whole bottle.

She giggles. "No, silly, I'm in second grade."

"Really? I never would've guessed. What's your favorite subject?"

Emma holds up her hand, ticking each one off. "Math, Science, Social Studies, Art, Music, Writing, Computers, and Library."

"What about lunch, recess, and gym?" I take another sip, trying to conceal my smile of amusement. This girl is too much.

"Lunch is good, recess can be boring, and gym…" She sticks out her tongue. "…I hate it."

"You don't hate anything," Jules is quick to correct her. "You don't care for it."

Emma spins in her mom's arms. "No, I hate it. You have to take off your shoes, and everyone's feet stink. Mean old P.J. never wears matching socks, then you have to run and even dribble a ball sometimes. Kids laugh at you when you do it wrong. It's lame and I hate it."

"Emma Jane, what am I going to do with you?"

Max enters the house again with the journal and Finn's pencil in his hand. He sets it next to him. Finn grabs it, opening it up to the page he was looking for and scribbles down his thought. Then he's back to building and Emma is at it too, making a kingdom for her stuffed animals to keep the mean ones away.

There's not near enough room in the chair for Max. It seems he doesn't care as he wiggles in right next to me. I end up sitting on half of him. He takes the wine glass from my hand, sniffs it, and takes a tiny sip.

"Oh, you must be in good with ol' Momma right there. She's sharing her favorite with you."

"It's delicious," I announce.

Jules moves closer to us, settling in a recliner. "I don't know what I'm going to do with her. She loves school but seriously struggles in the social department. She marches to her own drum, that one."

"She's amazing. Honestly, most kids her age have a hard time fitting in. The best thing is letting her be her."

"I was nervous about tonight for several reasons." She points to the two kids. "That being most of it. I wasn't sure how it would all go."

"Pretty damn perfect from the looks of it." Max squeezes me tight.

And he's right, it has been a perfect evening. I just can't forget my boots are upstairs. The memory of what happened up there warms my insides.

"You want another?" Jules points to the glass.

I nod, having no self-discipline. It's a common theme—I indulge in everything way too much when I'm around Max. Jules returns with two glasses of wine then shuffles back into the kitchen, reappearing with a plate of cookies.

Max has flipped on the television, turning it to Sports Center. It's muted as he reads the stats scrolling across the bottom and watches a basketball game.

"These are amazing. You'll have to share your recipe, Kate."

Max snorts, which earns him an elbow to the ribs. I start to open my mouth, but he beats me to the punch.

"Put your car in drive and head south for about fifteen miles until you run into a bakery on the main street."

Chapter 19

Kate

"You did amazing, babe." Max kisses the top of my head for the hundredth time and squeezes my hand.

My insides continue to shake, even though I seem fine from the outside. Moments ago, it was a whole different scene. My voice quaked with nerves and tears spilled over as I stood in front of the school board and told my story. The interim superintendent, elementary principal, and new school board president were all present to hear it. It took me three weeks to get there.

Jessie's parents and Cody sat in the back for support, along with Max. Whit and Jack watched the two younger kids in my room. I have no doubt it's going to be destroyed.

After all the incriminating evidence was laid out and my lawyer set up our plan of action if this wasn't corrected, the school board moved to pull the write-ups from my file. It was refreshing, and gut-wrenching, that it had to come down to this. Documentation and me saving all the texts were solid proof they couldn't turn down.

I didn't think Max was going to make it. At the very last minute, he slipped into the small room. That was the moment I relaxed just a tick, knowing he was standing behind me.

"She didn't show," he whispers as we walk down the hallway to my classroom.

"She didn't?" I whip my attention up to him.

"We waited the entire scheduled time. Harriet and the counselor played it off like they had missed her. Finn never brought up the fact Ally didn't come."

My heart is wounded for the little man. He has to be hurt. She is his mother, even after everything she's done to him.

"How is he?" I ask.

"Fine on the outside. He rolled his eyes when he saw Emma and growled a little about how obnoxious she was, but then he was showing her around his classroom."

"I'm telling you those two are going to be trouble, Max."

I was right; my classroom is destroyed. There are two happy children in the middle of the chaos.

"Who wants pizza?" Jessie announces when he follows us into the destruction zone.

"Me!" Emma jumps up, running over to her dad.

"Go clean up, then we'll go."

Finn looks up from his desk and smiles then goes back to writing in his journal. He keeps his eyes on the page as he frantically jots something down. "Dad,

I need three and a half minutes."

"You got it." Max begins helping his little sister pick up the mess.

There was a break-through the night we went to Max's parents for dinner. Finn was exposed to new people and an environment in which he thrived. It was when Finn thanked Max for his journal on the car ride home. Jules never commented on how bratty Finn had seemed. She kept her opinion to herself. It totally came across that way. But once Finn's mind was released from the one-way track of thought, he set it on thanking Max. It was everything.

The room almost looks normal in a matter of minutes.

"Your room is amazing," Jules comments.

"Thank you. It's my home away from home."

"Load up," Jessie announces.

The older kids are already outside with their faces plastered to their phones. Emma squeals and Finn closes his journal, having had enough time to finish whatever he was doing.

"Can I ride with Max? Please, please?" Emma clasps her hands in front of her chest, hopping up and down.

Finn grunts, but the smile on his face tells another story.

"Honey, there's not enough room. Where would Kate sit?" Jules asks.

Emma's excitement falls flat on the ground.

"I'll ride with you guys, and Emma can have my seat," I announce before tears start.

"Yes." Emma fist pumps the air. "Thank you, Kate."

"Come on, Finn." She grabs his hand and leads him outside.

"Trouble. I'm telling you all, and for the record, I predicted it first," I say.

Laughter ensues as we exit the building. Jessie orders enough pizza to feed the town. He knows what his family likes and doesn't have to ask. I noticed he leaned down and whispered in Finn's ear. He whispered right back, and I know that's why a large cheese pizza with extra cheese and a bottle of ketchup show up at our table.

Emma claps her hands when a pepperoni one shows up. The pepperonis spell out her name. Max and I fight over the Sour Pig.

"Finn, do you want a pepperoni from the E on my pizza? It's the most important letter in the alphabet, you know."

Finn curls his lip. "No, it's not. There's not one more important than the other. We have to have all of them."

"No sir, E is the best."

Finn rolls his eyes and takes the offered gift. He glides it through the ketchup before putting it in his mouth. The bell above the door rings, and we all turn to see Cody striding in. The older kids groan and protest that now there won't be any leftovers.

They are right. Cody puts down slice after slice, not caring what kind he inhales. I relax back in the booth, and Max's arm comes down around my shoulders. I lay my head on his chest.

"This is perfect," I whisper.

"It is."

I glance down at my freed wrist, thankful I got rid

of that clunker of a cast. I'm good as new in so many ways. I first notice Jessie stiffen, then Cody follows suit. It's not long before Max sits up to attention.

"Kids, let's go wash up then we can get ice cream." Jules stands, ushering Emma and Finn out of the booth. They go without a protest because—I mean—ice cream.

I'm the last to notice what everyone else already has. I blame it on my high on life and love stupor. When I see, I wish I could've remained in my perfect world. The reality is that Ally ripped that right away from me.

She's with the same filthy, nasty man. She hasn't noticed us yet as they talk to someone in the corner. Their voices rise with each word that's spoken.

"I don't have your stuff. Ally, you need to go home."

"That was my dead grandma's china and jewelry. You stole it."

Max discovered the reason Ally was looming back around her hometown. Her grandma passed, and she was back to collect what she thought was owed to her. It's really an easy equation. Money equals drugs.

The man stands from the booth. "You were evicted from the property and chose to leave everything behind."

Whoever the man is plays this out smart, walking out of the pizza place, not entertaining Ally's demands. She slams her foot down and goes for the door but not before she spots us in the corner. A hellacious laugh escapes her.

In this moment, my heart sinks for Ally. She's

fallen even further down the endless pit she'd spiraled into. In the short time since we ran into her on the sidewalk, her eyes have sunken in even more. She looks like she hasn't slept for days. Open sores cover the right side of her face, and she can't seem to stand still. Her hands move in rapid succession as she bounces from foot to foot.

"Jimmy," Cody calls out, then gives the guy behind the counter some sort of signal.

Ally seems to pick up on this, knowing exactly what it means. I'm assuming Cody just had the guy call the cops. Ally refuses to give in without a final word.

"Where is he?" she screams across the restaurant. "Where is my son?"

Max doesn't answer her, nor does anyone else at the table.

"He's mine." She beats her chest. "If you won't give him back, I'll take him. I need him. He's the only way I can get money now."

This last comment sets Max on fire. He's up and out of the booth before I realize what is happening. Cody and Jessie act fast, grabbing Max by his arms and yanking him back.

"You stupid, worthless bitch."

"Oh no." She covers her mouth. "Gutter trash turned town prince is a little pissy."

"Ally, let's go. They called the cops." The man wraps his greasy hands around her tiny arm and drags her out.

"I'm going to k—"

Jessie yanks Max back before he can finish his thought. "Not here, son."

191

"Fuck this." He jerks free. "I'm no longer a pawn in anyone's game, and my son won't be either."

Max storms out of the pizza place. I slide from the booth, but I'm too late when the door to the restaurant slams shut. Cody is hot on his heels.

"Let him go," Jessie says.

I know he's right, but staying here might be the hardest thing I've ever done. And the fact he's with Cody doesn't settle the tension at all. If Max wants whiskey, I know Cody won't blink twice giving it to him.

"I'll go get Mom from the bathroom," Whit announces.

"He's going to get drunk." The honest fear escapes before I realize it.

Jessie runs a hand over his hair then massages the back of his neck. "Have faith, Kate, have faith."

"We are ready!" Emma announces, prancing over to us.

Finn looks around for a second before his eyes go wide. "Where's my dad?" He turns around. His voice grows louder each time. "Dad. Dad. Dad."

"Hey." I rush over to him, dropping to my knees. "He went back to the school because I forgot to turn off a light. I gave him my key card to get in. He'll be back."

"You didn't forget to turn off your light. I saw you."

Finn has never been angry with me until this moment. He tries to shove away from me, but I don't let him.

"It's the room we had our meeting in. The one right next to the music room, Finn." I'm dying inside as the next lie slips from my mouth. "I promise. He's going to meet us at the ice cream shop, okay?"

He shakes his head. The hurt and pain on his face is enough to cripple me.

"Come on, Finn." Emma grabs his hand. "Mom said we can get as many scoops as we want."

The glare Finn shoots my way as he walks off crushes me. I tug my phone from my purse and text Max. I don't dare call him, knowing damn well Finn will be studying every one of my movements.

Me: Max we need you. Finn had a freak out when you weren't here.

Me: Please don't let her get to you. She'll never have Finn. He needs you right now.

My fingers tremble as I type. I can barely get out a whole thought before hitting send.

Me: I told him you went back to the school to turn off the lights in the room where we had the meeting. Heading to ice cream. We need you. Come back to us.

We don't even make it a half-block away before my phone begins ringing. Jessie, who is holding Emma's hand, and Jules, who is holding Finn's, both look back at me. My shoulders sag when I see Max's name on the screen.

"Hello."

"Hey, on my way. Is he okay?"

"Yes and no."

193

"Let me talk to him."

"Finn." I hold the phone up. "It's for you."

He swipes it from me. "Dad."

I can't hear what Max is saying on the other end. Finn nods and wipes away a stray tear.

"Dad, please hurry." Finn hands the phone back to me. The call has already ended, and I'm left feeling…I don't know what I'm feeling right now. We barely make it to the counter when the door to the ice cream shop swings wide open. I'm on edge, not so sure Ally won't still be creeping around. I'm hoping the thought of the cops being called will keep her the hell away.

"Finn." Max rushes in.

He looks like shit, frantic as hell with sweat beads on his forehead. I notice the smear of blood covering his knuckles. Finn darts to him, leaping up into his chest, burying his face in the crook of his neck.

"Why did you leave me?" Finn's muffled question is barely audible.

"Just ran to the school, buddy. I'd never leave you. Kate was with you and Jessie and Jules, and who could forget Emma?"

"Hey." She props a hand on her hip. "Let's order ice cream."

Emma starts off the long line of orders. Finn orders his from the safety of his dad's arms.

"Kate, you want anything?" Jessie asks.

I wave him off. "I ate too much at dinner."

The truth is I feel like I could puke at any moment. What I really want is to go home, curl up in a ball, and cry. I'm so pissed off at Max right now I'm not sure I can even look at him, much less enjoy ice cream. His reaction has me dumbstruck.

I get he has a temper when pushed, but to run out on Finn like that was bullshit. Yeah, he had all of us with him, but what happens when this happens and it's just Finn and Max?

I take a seat while the others wait for the young teens to scoop out their dessert. I'm being irrational, and I know it. Max would never leave Finn alone, no matter how pissed and raging he was. I just can't handle Ally and the way she can so easily disturb our lives.

I battle the instinct to react on my anger and try to remind myself to process this.

"Can I sit with you?" Whit asks, pointing to the single chair across from me.

I nod. "How did you manage to beat Emma through the line?"

Whit blushes. She's such a different girl than the one I met weeks ago. After witnessing the damage Ally has done to this family, I wholeheartedly understand her defense mechanism when we first met.

"Zack," she simply replies with a blush coating her cheeks.

"Zack?"

"Don't be obvious like my mom, but he's behind the counter with black hair."

I pretend to glance over at Max and Finn and get a perfect view of this Zack.

"Oh, Zack." I hum and smile.

"Don't tell my parents, especially my dad. It will get so ugly in here."

I laugh. "This is awesome. Tell me more. I need

195

to hear something good after tonight."

Whit sets down her bowl of bubblegum ice cream. "First, I need to apologize to you for being a total bitch when I first met you."

"Trust me, I get it now. No worries." I wave her off. "But cussing and telling me juicy secrets, take it easy on me here."

She giggles, then proceeds to tell me everything about Zack Montgomery. He's the star quarterback of their rival school. She's the head cheerleader of her school. Her dad would hurt him and then lock her away is repeated several times during the description. And in the end, I realize Whit is madly and deeply in love.

The rest of the family has settled in with their ice cream. Finn remains latched onto Max as he eats his chocolate tower of ice cream. Max helps him every once in a while, taking a spoonful for himself. My raging uncontrollable emotions rear their ugly head. I want to be by their side. I focus back on Whit.

"Is he your first?"

Her face goes pale.

"Love, Whit. Is he your first love, crush, or whatever the kids are calling it these days?"

She relaxes with the color coming back to life in her cheeks. And in perfect time, since Zack saunters over to the table next to us with a rag, cleaning an already pristine tabletop. Googly-eyed stares are shared for the briefest of moments before he walks away.

"He smells so good," she gushes.

All I smell is the cold scent of sweet frozen treats.

"He has a nice butt," I add. "Eeewww, no, that

was so wrong. I was trying to be hip and cool, and that pushed the limits. Gah."

Whit and I burst out in laughter. My stomach flexes in pain, the joyful kind, and tears roll down both our faces.

"Yeah, just a bit creepy." Whit holds up two fingers, leaving a tiny space between them.

"What's so funny down there?" Jessie asks.

"Yeah, what's so funny, sis?" Jack chirps.

He knows and he's holding it over her, but Whit isn't one to back down.

"The fact I'm making you ride the school bus tomorrow instead of with me to school."

Jack retracts really fast. Jules flicks her gaze to the counter, knowing damn well what is going on. Whit schools me on trends, the cool words to use, and words not to use. I'm still in awe "radical" is on the "do not say it ever" list. That was cool as shit when I was her age.

"Thanks for the pizza." I hug Jules and Jessie and even Whit. I get a chin jerk from Jack and pat Emma's back, who had crashed in her daddy's arms.

"And I'll see you two tomorrow." I wink at Max and awkwardly hug Finn, who is still clinging to his father.

"Where are you going?" Max asks, shocked.

"Just gonna walk back to the school, grab my car, and go home."

"No, you're not."

I nod. "Yeah, I am. I'm exhausted. Finn needs to get to bed. I'll see you tomorrow."

I wave and walk off before he can stop me. Max has his family to part with and Finn in his arms, leaving no way he can protest or stop me. The truth is I need space right now. Whit was the perfect distraction to neutralize my emotions, which happen to be all over the place right now.

In that short time, my anger has transformed into sorrow and bitterness. Not toward Max or Finn, but aimed directly at Ally. She has no idea how much power she holds over them. She doesn't give a shit either. She's fixed on one thing and one thing only: getting her next high.

It's all too much, and I just need a timeout. My phone dings when I get to my car, alerting me to a text.

Max: Did you make it to your car? I'm not very happy with you right now.

Me: I'm fine and in my car.

Max: I'm coming to the school once I get Finn buckled in.

Me: Don't. I'm tired and going home.

Max: What the hell, Kate? Are you mad?

Me: I'm not pleased. I'm tired. Good night.

I barely get the final word typed out before my screen goes black. That's what happens when you don't charge it after twelve hours. The streets are deserted as I drive home. My porch light is on and my bed is calling my name. I unlock the front door, step inside, lock it back up and kick off my shoes.

I feel horrible about my texts when I see the vase of wildflowers on my dining room table, the ones Max and Finn picked for me a few nights ago. I skip washing my face and climbing into pajamas. I strip down to my panties and tug on a t-shirt before plugging in my phone and waiting for it to power on.

My eyelids grow heavy as I wait for the phone to get enough juice to come back to life. I'm about to drift away into peace when a loud clang startles me to life. I leap from the bed and clutch my chest. It takes me long moments to realize it's my phone making the noise as my notifications flow in.

It must have been the fact I was moments before entering dreamland that startled me. There are six texts from Max. I don't read them; instead, I call him.

"Hello," he whispers into the phone.

"Hey, you get Finn down?"

"Yeah, just creeping out of his room."

"Oh." All of a sudden I'm at a loss for words.

"You're pissed at me," he states.

I slap a hand on my forehead. "I don't know what I am, Max."

"I shouldn't have left."

"No, you shouldn't have. It hurt."

"She knows how to push my buttons."

I exhale loudly and brave his anger to speak the next words. "I get that. What I'm struggling with is you letting her. Is this going to be how it always is? It's complicated and nasty. I get that. She threatens taking Finn away every time and knows just how to make your old scars burn to life."

"Kate," he tries to interrupt.

"No, Max, I'm not done. I'm hurt because I love Finn and I love you. You know this, yet you took her bait so easily then stormed out tonight. It's not okay."

There's silence, so I continue.

"Finn deserves better. I deserve better and so do you."

"What are you saying, Kate? You're scaring the hell out of me."

"You need to work harder on you, Max."

"Are you leaving me?" His voice cracks on the last part.

"No, but I won't be around much longer if tonight ever repeats itself." I pause. "I love you and want all of you, every single second of the day."

"I get it." He lets out a huff of air. "Dad chewed my ass, too."

"Good." I smile.

"You walking away from me tonight scared the shit out of me, Kate. Don't ever do that again, please."

"Don't make me feel like I did tonight, and I won't."

"How did you feel?"

"Hopeless."

"Jesus, baby, I'm so sorry."

I yawn into the phone. Not lady-like at all.

"Get some sleep. I'll have coffee over to you in the morning. Love you, Kate."

"Love you, too, Max."

I end the call feeling better about getting my mixed-up emotions off my chest. It's healthier than letting them take up space and fester. It's not long before my eyelids close and I have a smile on my face.

"Life doesn't have to be perfect to be wonderful," I whisper to myself.

Right before I'm about to drift to sleep, a strong odor invades my room. I gag when I sit up. Gasoline? What in the hell?

"Get her valuables. I'll take care of her."

Am I caught in a nasty nightmare?

Voices stream into my bedroom. I scramble for the phone. The door bursts open, startling a scream from me, deep down low. My phone crashes to the floor.

"Hello, Kate."

Chapter 20

Max

"You gotta keep that shit in, man," Cody says, kicking his feet up on the table. "You're damn lucky she's even talking to you right now."

"I know." I scrub my face. "Ally gets to me every fucking time."

"You still seeing that shrink?"

"Not as regular as I should."

"Thinking that should be your first step."

Cody showed up at my front door when I hung up with Kate.

"Thanks, Cody. Wasn't any way I was going to get sleep anytime soon."

He waves me off, tipping back a beer. "Love is a funny thing. It can build up and destroy in a blink of an eye."

"What's your story? Make me feel better. Dad only ever told me you had your heart broken and wasn't even sure if you still had one, besides the fact you're alive."

"Nothing I'm proud of and ain't much to tell. Was in love hard. She was my world. I was young and dumb and horny. That part hasn't changed. She pissed me off, and her slutty roommate was there. Made the biggest mistake of my life. She left town and never returned."

I chug the remaining water in the bottle. "You go after her?"

"Naw." He shakes his head. "There was no excuse for what I did. Deserved the punishment."

"That's brutal, man."

"It's life." He gets up to grab another beer from the six-pack he brought over. "Now let's quit being pussies here. You got any porn or shoot 'em up flicks we can pass the time with?"

I shake my head. "Jesus, Cody, I ain't watching porn with you."

We find something on Netflix that satisfies Cody. I watch the show then go flip through my phone, looking at pictures of Kate and Finn, vowing to never walk out on what's important in my life again, no matter what the circumstance. A smile turns up the corner of my lips when I see the picture of Kate adjusting her glasses while trying to read the instructions on a brownie mix box. The next one is of her asleep on my pillow. Her wild mane of blonde hair swirls around her shoulders, her lips are relaxed, and her hand rests on my chest in the bottom part of the picture. Then there's one of her and Finn holding hands on one of our nighttime strolls.

I nod off to sleep, with the sound of the television in the background and thoughts of my little family filling my dreams. The way it should be.

An alarm blares, causing me to leap from my recliner. Cody does the same thing from the couch where he must have drifted off to sleep, too. The light from the TV flickers in the background.

"What in the hell is going on?"

"There's a fire." Cody slips into his boots.

"What? Where?" My foggy, sleep-riddled brain can't keep up. It hits me that Cody is head of the volunteer firefighters here in town.

"In town a few blocks over." Cody darts for the door and freezes in his tracks when he realizes what he's said. He turns to me. "Max."

"What's the address?" I grit out.

"Stay here. You can't leave. I'll keep you updated." He sprints out the door and into the darkness.

"What's the address?" I roar.

He doesn't answer, peeling away in his truck. I look towards Kate's house to see the glow of a fire and smoke billowing toward the full moon.

"No, no, no."

"Dad?" I turn in the doorway leading out to the porch to see Finn wiping the sleep from his eyes. "What's going on?"

My world is ending, I think to myself.

"Nothing, bud. Cody fell asleep here and had to leave."

"What time is it?" He yawns wide.

"Let's go back to bed, son."

My phone rings in the living room. I race to get it, hoping like hell to see Kate's name. My hope evaporates when Dad's pic and name race across the screen.

"Hey," I answer, guiding Finn back to his room.

"We are on our way. Cody called us. Mom will stay with Finn. You wait until we get there."

"Dad."

"Max, listen to me. We don't know anything yet. Stay at the house."

I drop the phone to the bed and help Finn in.

"You forgot to push the button, Dad." He picks it up and ends the call. Once he's snuggled back in the blankets, he begins to drift off but not before he crushes me.

"Dad, can Kate be my mom?"

I brush back his hair and kiss his forehead. "She sure can, and I know she'd love it."

"Love you, Dad."

I don't get the chance to repeat the words back to him before he's sound asleep. I don't move until I hear Dad's truck pull up. I creep from the bed, numb and scared as hell. Mom meets me in the hallway.

"He's asleep. Shouldn't wake up until around six forty-five." My voice is flat.

"Max, everything will be all right."

I want to scream or punch something because nothing will ever be the same. I don't need to know the exact address of the house fire to know it was Kate's. That thought snaps me back to life. I'm out the front door and in the front seat of Dad's truck. He doesn't say a word as he hauls ass the few short blocks to Kate's.

Fire trucks, ambulances, and cop cars make it impossible to get near her home. I leap from the truck and take off sprinting. The once-quaint home blazes in a fiery inferno.

"Hey, get back here," someone yells. I don't stop until I'm in the middle of the chaos screaming for answers.

It's as if no one hears my cries for help. They go unanswered. Dad is at my side doing the same, but we get nothing. It feels like an eternity before a police officer even acknowledges our presence.

"There was a woman in there. Has she been found?" Dad asks, getting right up in his face.

The officer shakes his head. "I can't tell you anything, sir…"

I cut him off. "She's my girlfriend. I know she was in there. Are you searching for her?"

Four gunshots pop into the night air. At first, I think it's the house crumbling, but I'd know a gunshot anywhere. I grab my dad and duck, then realize they are too far away for them to be any danger.

"The two suspects are down." The announcement streams from the officer's radio. "Shot to kill when one fired off a gun of their own."

The officer presses his mic. "It's confirmed there's one individual in the house. I repeat, it's confirmed there's one individual in the house."

"We've got our men in there. Only a few more minutes before I pull them."

Dad grabs a firefighter racing by. "Sam, who's in there? Have they found her? Is there any communication?"

He shakes his head. "Cody busted in there."

The grim look on his face tells us everything we need to know.

Chapter 21

Kate

"He's a good boy."

I blink once then twice.

"I was a horrible mother. Hurt him worse than anything possibly could. But he's found you and Jessie and Jules. Even though I was evil, God answered my prayers. I just wanted my baby boy protected because I know I was nothing but evil."

"Who are you?"

"Max's momma."

"Kate, can you hear me?" I'm being lifted up. "Kate, can you hear me?"

They need to stop screaming at me. I just want to sleep. I open my mouth to tell them so, only to find there's no oxygen left in my lungs.

***

Max

I pace the halls. Energy flows through me. After the six-hour drive to the hospital where Cody and Kate were life-flighted, I can't sit still. Dad hasn't moved from where he's been leaning up against a wall.

"We don't have a pulse," are the last words I heard when Kate was put in the back of the ambulance.

No one here will give me any kind of information since I'm not next of kin. I've kept my stare on the doors leading to the operating rooms. The sun has risen and is threatening to go back down with no word on the condition of either of them.

I FaceTime with Finn, giving him the tiniest of details. All he knows is Kate had an accident and that I have to be with her. Only if I can be with her.

At that moment, the doors swing wide open. I'm bound and determined to get answers, no matter the cost.

"Kate. I need to know about Kate Wilson-Valentukonis. I'm her fiancé. Her parents have been contacted but are out of the country with no cell service. She has no siblings. I'm all she has."

The surgeon pulls the cap from his head and balls it in his hands while shaking his head. I feel my dad lift me up from the back because my legs go out on me. My world spins, and I'm throttled into darkness.

"Max."

I hear my name but can't come to.

"Max." This time, a harsh slap accompanies my name, bringing me back.

"There you are, son. Jesus, don't be doing that to me. She's alive."

I'm on my feet, wobbling from side to side.

"Sit back down." Dad pushes me down. "She's alive and recovering from surgery."

"Surgery?"

Dad nods his head.

"I want all the details, now."

"She was beaten badly. The doctors are guessing who ever did this…"

"Ally," I interrupt.

"…figured she was dead." Dad sits back down. "The cops told us the house was set on fire. Cody got to her in time."

"Surgery," I repeat again.

"Her jaw was broken, and she has a collapsed lung, traumatic damage to her abdomen, and severe swelling on her brain. She's pulling through, Max. Her lungs are in the worst shape, from smoke inhalation and being collapsed."

I'm unable to process any of it.

"Cody saved her life. Got to her in time."

"Cody, Jesus."

"You worry about one thing at a time."

I nod, unable to blink from shock.

"You can go see her, Max."

Dad guides me to the intensive care unit. The massive hospital bed swallows up Kate's tiny figure. Tubes and wires go in every direction. A steady thumping sound beats in the room. Whooshing accompanies the sound as machines help Kate breathe.

I go to her side and crumble, clutching her hand.

"Kate, oh my God, Kate."

Not one shred of anger courses through me at the thought this all happened at Ally's hands. I'm brought to my knees clinging to Kate's hand, and I pray like I've never prayed before. I repeat the words over and over.

I don't leave her side. One day, then two, and eventually five pass by with no signs of improvement. I hold her hand the entire time, only leaving to use the bathroom and spend a few minutes with Finn in the waiting room.

Doctors grow more dismal as each day passes by. I can't help it, but in the quiet times I stare at Kate's belly. She was pregnant. Not that far along, but we had created a tiny miraculous life that was ripped away from us.

If Ally and her partner weren't announced dead the night of the fire, I'd be pounding the pavement in search of her in order to take her life. I'd bathe my knuckles in their blood and feel no remorse at all. Their greed and addiction ruined so many lives. Ally's fatal and final mistake of raising a gun and firing at an officer cost her life and the man she travelled with. It was nothing less than a blessing that officer only suffered a surface bullet wound.

"Son, Mom has dinner and Finn out in the waiting room. Go take a break."

I don't speak unless I have to, and this is a time I don't. I have no more energy left to put on a happy *all is good* face for Finn. I'm a hollow man.

"Dad." Finn runs up to me when I enter the room. I hug him tight.

"Grandma said no, but…"

He started calling Jules "Grandma" over the last few days. Should make me happy as hell and proud, but it doesn't.

"Finn," Mom warns.

"But," he continues, "I want to see Kate, please."

"Do the hand thing and jump up and down," Emma tries to whisper.

Finn follows her instructions. "I miss Kate. Please, Dad. I can tell her stories and remind her of all her students. It will work. She loves us."

I scrub my face, not knowing what to tell him. Seeing Kate in this state will scar him forever. I don't want his last memory of her being laid up in a bed, lifeless. He needs to remember the full of life, loving Kate who saved him.

"Dad, it will work." He frantically nods his head.

The sheer hope in his words are foreign. It's been missing since the day I saw her in that bed.

"Sure, why not?" I sit him down and go over what to expect and that Kate won't talk back.

I squeeze his shoulders as I walk him back to the room. The nurses don't kick Dad out, even though there's a strict two-visitor policy.

"Lift me up, Dad." Finn raises his arms.

He winces when Kate's face comes into view. But he's on a mission, wiggling out of my arms and settling on the bed next to Kate. He manages to lie down next to her, avoiding all the tubes. He pets her hair gently. I'm forced to turn away because this is the final straw that will break me.

"Oh, Miss Kate, I'm sorry about your face," he coos to her. "Dad finally let me see you. I've been wanting to tell you things. First, I love you, Miss

211

Kate. Second, will you be my mom? Third, you have to wake up or Mrs. Bradshaw will be our substitute for the rest of the year. She has warts and smells. She doesn't like me. I don't think she likes any of the kids. You have to wake up."

I face my brave and courageous son, going to his side.

Finn perches up on his elbows. "Are you waking up?"

His face falls in a frown.

"I hate fairytales. They're dumb. You know this, but Emma said Dad needs to kiss you like in *Sleeping Beauty* and you'll open your eyes. Dad." He looks up at me.

I find a smile dancing on my lips. "I got this."

I bend down, whispering my love for Kate before sealing my lips to hers.

***

Kate

I hear you, Finn. I'm right here, trying hard to wake up. Oh, his sweet words have me fighting hard. *Yes, I'll be your mom.* I want to scream. The harder I try to open my eyes, the more weight rests on them.

I'm here, Finn. I hear you. I repeat it over and over in my head. It's been dark and cold forever. I feel his warmth seeping in and crave it like no other. *Come on, body.*

"I got this." Max's deep voice seeps in.

He whispers his love to me, then the warmth I've been seeking flows from my roots right down to my toes. I pray he never leaves. He's bringing me back to life.

Something in my throat causes me to gag. I'm choking, coughing, and spluttering. My eyes fly open, and the light blinds me. I can't breathe again. I panic, coughing harder and fighting to get just a gasp of air.

"She's awake," I hear someone yell. "She's awake."

Finn is a blur as he's jerked away from the bed. Random faces stare down at me. In one swift movement, I'm able to take in air. I try to talk, but there are razor blades of some sort lining my throat.

I thrash in the bed, reaching for my boys, only to have my arms put back down by my side.

"I'm here, Mommy. We are here," Finn's sweet voice hollers out over the chaos. I focus on it while gulping in air.

They're here.

I'm here.

Max's mom's prayers were answered.

Epilogue

"She's fat."

"She's not fat. She's growing my brother or sister."

"And that's why she's fat."

I peer through my legs at Emma and Finn debating over my body while I'm in my final yoga pose.

"She's right, Finn. I'm fat. One big Butterball turkey of fat."

"Emma Jane," Jules hollers from the kitchen. "What did I tell you?"

"She's not fat. She's pregnant."

Finn gives her a victorious "I told you so" head jerk. I go down to my knees and roll over on my back, exhausted from yoga and being nine months pregnant. Max told me there was no way in hell I'd be able to keep up with yoga all nine months, hence why I'm about to die.

I take a silent moment to smooth my hands over my belly. I was told conceiving and then being able to carry a baby to full-term would be impossible due to the trauma of being beaten, taking most of the brutal kicks to my stomach which caused internal damage and led to surgeries and scarring around my uterus. Not one inch of the flames touched me that horrific night. Cody was my shield.

"Get your busy butts in here and help finish the pies," Jules hollers in her mean mom voice. "Let Kate have her moment of zen or whatever."

I smile at the kids' defeated looks. Emma hops right up, leaving her disaster of Legos behind. Finn chews on his bottom lip, debating his next move. He reaches for a block then scrunches his tiny fist together.

"Damn, tacos." He huffs and stands, joining his cousin.

She's actually his aunt, but we've settled on them being cousins. We moved in with Jessie and Jules during the months I spent recovering. I pushed my body back, not wasting one second. I never finished out the school year teaching but still spend plenty of hours volunteering.

And even though it's winter and there're feet of snow outside, Max and Jessie are working on a house. Max picked his favorite spot on the farm and poured a foundation. Until the house is finished, we are living with Jessie and Jules. I have to admit, I have it made with Jules taking care of us. It's going to be a rude awakening when I'm in charge of my own household.

We made a family decision to homeschool Finn and Emma. They both were being held back in the public school system, at no fault to anyone. Having essentially a classroom of two students is amazing

215

and fun. We go at our own pace and even take long road trips learning about science and geography.

The chaos in the kitchen grows louder. I hear Jessie and Max enter. And then before I know it, Max stands above me.

"Rough day?" He smirks, knowing damn well I hate yoga at this point.

"Shut your mouth when you're talking to me."

He reaches out a hand, and I take it. It's always my favorite part of the day when my hand is wrapped in his.

"Go shower, Jessie. Brady is picking up Cody and then heading here for dinner."

"Then presents," Emma squeals.

"Come wash my back," Jessie responds to Jules.

Both kids squeal out their disgust, gaining a chuckle from Jessie.

Cody is still healing from his burns. He tends to crawl into himself. The bar is on the verge of closing, and he can't seem to muster up one ounce of giving a shit. The thing is his family, us, won't allow it. He gets dragged to everything he can handle. Hell, he even showed some excitement at Emma and Finn's soccer game this fall. Well, that was until they were both politely asked to leave their team due to their lack of interest and Emma's knack for starting arguments.

As Max helps me to my feet, the twinkle of the Christmas tree catches my attention. It's truly the most magical time of the year. We've been blessed beyond belief. I used to think I was lucky. This, everything around me, has nothing to do with luck. I catch the twinkle of the angel on the top of the tree and repeat the same prayer I say every day for Cody and his soul.

"You stink." Max sniffs my neck. "Come wash my back."

I slap his ass as he leads me up the stairs to his childhood bedroom. My due date is tomorrow. I have the man I love. A son. A family who is crazy and amazing. I have everything a woman could wish for except my little girl. I rub the miracle inside of me. My swollen belly is proof that anything can happen. I wasn't supposed to be able to get pregnant again. They told me I'd never carry a baby to full term.

And here I am.

Epilogue Part 2

"I should be an author on the cover." Emma remains in her position with her hands on her hips.

"You didn't write anything." Finn doesn't look up from the stack of books in front of him.

"I've already sold all the copies, got us into the local craft show, and was able to copy the first book in Dad's office."

I'm distracted from the banter in front of me by soft kisses to my temple. I smile over at Max, feeling high on life. Emma and Finn are battling over their math project. An English assignment turned into Finn publishing his beloved journal. Emma gave up on her picture book about frogs and princes and became engrossed in Finn's journal. I've got to admit I really had no idea what was in it, and when I saw a few pages ready to edit and offer up constructive criticism, I was left speechless.

It's the tale of a little boy who ticks to a different beat from his view. Finn didn't leave out any of the good memories with Francis to the scary nights with

Ally and when he found his daddy. There were random doodles of blocks and foreign subjects. What Max and I didn't know was every time he was building with blocks, he was telling his story and how he saw the world.

Max never wanted to test Finn. Instead, we both decided to focus on developing coping skills with him. It hasn't been easy, but it gets better every day. Even though he's homeschooled, he explores more things than he would if he was in the public school system. If we are studying ecosystems and habitats, we go to the pond and observe the area. The kids predict the type of fish inhabiting the pond, collect bugs, and make analyses.

"They're never going to settle this argument," Max whispers in my ear.

I peer over to him and smile. "All they have to do is figure out a profit and loss margin."

"Again, no way they will ever agree."

"And they're learning the greatest lesson of compromise and team work."

"One of them might lose an eye."

I shrug. "Possible."

Max shakes his head, capturing my lips in his. He kisses the hell out of me like he's always done. We don't part until a tiny squeak and wiggle in my arms breaks through.

We both peer down to our perfect baby, Jillian, all wrapped up in her pink blanket with her perfect lips pursed and rosy cheeks on display. I have no idea what we have in store with this little one. All I do know is she stormed in on Christmas Day and has been a perfect blessing ever since.

Max leans down, placing a kiss on her forehead. It guts me like it always does when he does this. It wasn't easy picking out a name for our baby girl. I'll never forget how nervous I was when I broached the subject of naming her after his mother. Of course, Max was pissed and wouldn't hear anything of it. I was prepared for him to storm off and return later cooled down. The thing is he hasn't done that since the night in the pizza place.

It took him a while to come around to it and a serious talk with his dad, Jessie. I went on to explain to him about the dream I had. I've never admitted to anyone that it was more than a dream. I met his mother and saw the sorrow and pain in her eyes. She was so happy for Max, but there was so much redemption that would never happen lingering in her eyes.

It came down to the fact that Max would've never met me if it hadn't been for his mom. It was the years of hardship he endured that led him into his future, which was set on a final destination straight to me. If Max would've led the high life like he deserved with loving parents, chances are he never would have caught Ally's eye. The truth is she never would've gone after Max if it weren't for the attention he was gaining after his mom died and Jessie took him in. Her game had always been an attention-seeking one; it wasn't an easy pill to swallow.

Jillian's namesake will forever be cherished in our hearts and in Max's mom's memory. The beauty in life is not hating, but rather respecting, where you come from no matter how ugly it is. And that's the same life lesson we are both on board to teach Finn.

"Enough." Jules enters the living room, settling next to Finn on the floor. "This is Finn's book. Yes, it was you, Emma, that snuck into your dad's office to copy the book and waste an entire forest, but he wrote it, honey."

I bite down on my smile, remembering when we were about to move into our new house and Emma pulled the biggest heist over us. We'd all thought she was sick running to the bathroom during our grammar lesson. Little did we know, she was sneaking into Jessie's office making a copy of the book. Finn is no innocent party sidetracking all of us while she was gone.

Jessie was fit to be tied when he went into his office, exhausted, to find a pile of crumpled papers mounded in the middle of the room. They were Emma's mistakes. And if I had to guess, it was nearly a ream of paper. The little shit even figured out how to change the ink cartridge when it ran out.

Finn glances up to Emma. "We can put your name as the publisher."

"They are already printed," she fires back, which makes no sense, since she is demanding to be co-author.

Finn scratches the side of his head. "Remember those labels we were going to order from Amazon on Grandma's account?"

"Finn!" Emma smacks her forehead.

He blushes and continues on. "Well, what if we ask this time and we can print your name as the publisher?"

Emma taps her chin in dramatic fashion. None of us would expect anything less. "Only if we put it on

221

the sign in front of Cody's bar, and my name has to be in all capital letters."

"Okay." Finn nods, not caring whether the sign happens or not.

Cody left New Year's Day. It's left a hole in our entire family unit. I find myself struggling with the fact he's going through hell because he saved me. My skin was never touched by the hot flames because of Cody. He gave everything to keep me safe. Cody is still healing and will for a long damn time. It was Jessie and Brady who gave him no choice and admitted him into a rehabilitation center.

At the time, nobody made him go. It wasn't until we all saw him slipping day by day that we knew he had to go. There's nothing worse than seeing the man who saved you diminish day by day. Every night his name is whispered on my lips. I give it all to God, knowing he'll find a way to heal the hero named Cody.

Jillian cries out in protest in Max's arms. The natural daddy he is, he does his best to soothe her.

"Here." I hold out my arms. "She wants Momma."

I lift the bottom of my shirt. Max places our perfect little girl in the precise position. Jillian latches her pursed lips around me and soothes right down. It's Max's hand cradling her head that makes the picture complete. I have everything, and even though we aren't in our brand new house and have decided to spend the night here, it adds to the abundance of our blessing.

Jessie bursts through the door, startling Jillian. It only takes a few strokes of Max's hand to relax her again.

"You are not going to the goddamn prom with the rival quarterback to my team."

"Dad!" Whit protests.

"Don't, Whit." He turns around. "I'm not going to even entertain this idea."

By this time, all attention is on the dueling pair in front of us. Jules jumps up, brushing her palms down the front of her yoga pants, encroaching on her pissed-off husband. She laces her hands around his middle.

"Honey, is this a bad time to tell you that Zack will be joining us tonight for family dinner?"

Jessie's jaw clenches. He doesn't say another word as he storms upstairs. The only sound of slamming doors echoes down. Whit tosses herself in Jessie's recliner.

"Mom, I told you he'd do this. It was no good easing him into the idea of it."

Jules walks over to her, perching on the arm of the chair and pulling her in for a hug. "It will be fine. You need to take it easy with Dad. Zack being the star quarterback to your dad's rival team is only salt in the wound."

Jillian fills her diaper once she's done nursing. I escape the chaos that's about to ensue. I feel for poor Whit; she has no chance of dating with Jessie and Max being her guard dogs. I sing a lullaby while changing Jillian's diaper and decide to change her outfit because it's just too much fun. And Lord knows Jules provides us with endless supplies of clothes. I feel guilty not using all of them, so I do my best.

There's a knock at the door when I walk down the stairs. Jessie answers the door, and there's no shock there. Whit is pale as a ghost. Jules shakes her head. Emma and Finn have no idea what's going on as they sort the printed books into piles on the floor while writing down totals on their columned paper.

Max is relaxed back on the couch, taking a sip of his whiskey with an amused look on his face. I settle next to him, elbowing him in the ribs and doing my best not to wake the milk-induced coma Jillian in my arms.

"Be good," I hiss to him.

"Not a chance," he replies, keeping his attention focused on the show that's about to go down.

"Sir," Zack extends his hand, "I'm Zack."

Jessie growls. Literally freaking growls like a rabid dog. Jules plays referee, racing to Zack's rescue, welcoming him in the home. Whit covers her face the entire time.

"Would you like anything to drink?" Jules asks.

"No, thank you, Ma'am."

Points for Zack. He really is a nice kid. I've become like Whit's trusted sounding board. There hasn't been one red flag to date.

Whit finally finds her voice and introduces Zack to everyone, then guides him to the couch to take a seat. I have to give it to Zack—he keeps his cool with all of the gazes and hostility streaming from Jessie.

Right before Whit is about to sit next to Zack, Jessie butts in, sitting right beside him. He pats the seat on the other side of him. Whit groans and takes it. Jessie spreads his arm wide on the back of the couch. Then there's silence. Deafening silence until

Zack clears his throat. He tries to twist a bit on the couch to face Jessie but really can't. The scene is beyond awkward. Whit remains strong, not bursting into tears when most girls her age would be a sobbing, embarrassed mess. It's the consequence and honor of being raised by a gentle giant who is way too protective.

"Sir, I came here to ask if I could take Whit to my prom." Zack's nerves get the best of him as his voice wavers just a tick.

"Nope. No way in hell," Jessie barks out.

"Jessie," Jules scolds him.

"Dad," Whit turns to him, "I really like Zack and would like to go."

"Nope." Jessie remains firm in his decision.

"What about going to your prom, Whit, with Zack?" Jules offers.

Jessie's jaw clenches. He can shoot down Zack like no other but is smart enough not to do it to his wife.

"I'd be okay with that," Zack replies.

"No," Whit protests. "That's not fine. Zack wants to take me to his. That's the question."

I go in for the kill, hoping it wouldn't come down to this. "I was talking to some of my friends I used to teach with, and they're looking for chaperones still. Max and I can be chaperones if that would make you feel any better, Jessie."

"That's a great compromise," Jules chimes in.

"Hey." Emma pops up from the floor, racing over to Zack. "You want to buy a book? They're five dollars." She waves one in front of his face.

"Twenty dollars," Jessie corrects her. "They are

225

twenty dollars."

Emma's puzzled look is priceless. Max told me about the expensive-as-hell lemonade Jessie made his team buy. I know his game here.

"The fool better get used to it," Max whispers in my ear.

Zack doesn't hesitate. "I'll take two."

"That's forty, mister." Emma holds out her hand.

Zack digs two crisp twenty-dollar bills from his pocket. Finn races over with the second book.

"Do you want it signed by the author and publisher?" Emma beams a wide smile.

"Sure." Zack nods.

"That's ten dollars extra," Jessie grumbles.

Zack doesn't hesitate, once again pulling more money from his wallet.

"That's enough, Jessie," Jules scolds.

Jessie doesn't move, keeping himself right in the middle of the conversation. After the books are signed and given to Zack, the awkward level escalates.

"Jessie, I need your help," Jules hollers from the kitchen where she escaped after the last of the money was exchanged.

He doesn't move or respond.

"Jessie, get your ass in here or we will be having words."

And just like that, Jessie gets up and nods to Max. He goes to stand and holy hell puts himself right between Whit and Zack, taking his dad's place.

I offer Whit a gentle smile and say, "It's about the little battles, not the war. You're going to the prom."

This makes Whit grin from ear to ear.

"You hold any records yet, boy?" Max asks, resting his arm around Zack's tense shoulders.

"No, sir."

"That's a shame, but then again gonna be pretty hard to beat any of mine. Hasn't been one Trojan player close to doing so."

I roll my eyes and gaze down at Jillian. She is so damn screwed. She has no chance of ever looking at a boy.

I look up to see Max staring at me. He knows exactly what I'm thinking and has audacity to grin at me.

Bonus!

Get Instant Access to A "Secret" Bonus Chapter From *That Was Yesterday* by HJ Bellus Now!

https://limitlesspublishing.lpages.co/that-was-yesterday/

Acknowledgments

Thank you for taking the time to read Max's story. You guys are my rock stars. I want to acknowledge all the amazing and selfless teachers, coaches, and role models out there. You never know when you might change the course of someone's life forever. There has been many in my life that I'll never forget. There's also been one in my daughter's life. This woman encouraged Libby to believe in herself and go for her goals. There will never enough words to express my gratitude. Brinkley, you'll always be a legend in the Hooper household.

About the Author

HJ Bellus is a small-town girl who loves the art of storytelling. When not making readers laugh or cry, she's a part-time livestock wrangler that can be found in the middle of Idaho, shot gunning a beer while listening to some Miranda Lambert on her Beats and rocking out in her boots.

Join my newsletter:
http://bit.ly/2Lwofma

Facebook:
https://www.facebook.com/AuthorHjBellus

Twitter:
https://twitter.com/HJBellus

Goodreads:
https://www.goodreads.com/HJBellus

Join our Reader Group on Facebook and don't miss out on meeting our authors and entering epic giveaways!

Limitless Reading

Where reading a book
is your first step to becoming
limitless...

Join today! *"Where reading a book is your first step to becoming limitless..."*

https://www.facebook.com/groups/LimitlessReading/